USA TODAY BESTSELLING AUTHOR

Dale Mayer

Flynn's FIRECRACKER

HEROES FOR HIRE

FLYNN'S FIRECRACKER: HEROES FOR HIRE, BOOK 5
Beverly Dale Mayer
Valley Publishing Ltd.

ISBN-13: 978-1-773360-35-5
Print Edition

Books in This Series:

Levi's Legend: Heroes for Hire, Book 1
Stone's Surrender: Heroes for Hire, Book 2
Merk's Mistake: Heroes for Hire, Book 3
Rhodes's Reward: Heroes for Hire, Book 4
Flynn's Firecracker: Heroes for Hire, Book 5
Logan's Light: Heroes for Hire, Book 6
Harrison's Heart: Heroes for Hire, Book 7
Saul's Sweetheart: Heroes for Hire, Book 8
Dakota's Delight: Heroes for Hire, Book 9
Tyson's Treasure: Heroes for Hire, Book 10
Jace's Jewel: Heroes for Hire, Book 11
Rory's Rose: Heroes for Hire, Book 12
Brandon's Bliss: Heroes for Hire, Book 13
Liam's Lily: Heroes for Hire, Book 14
North's Nikki: Heroes for Hire, Book 15
Anders's Angel: Heroes for Hire, Book 16
Reyes's Raina: Heroes for Hire, Book 17
Dezi's Diamond: Heroes for Hire, Book 18
Vince's Vixen: Heroes for Hire, Book 19
Ice's Icing: Heroes for Hire, Book 20
Johan's Joy: Heroes for Hire, Book 21
Galen's Gemma: Heroes for Hire, Book 22
Zack's Zest: Heroes for Hire, Book 23
Bonaparte's Belle: Heroes for Hire, Book 24
Noah's Nemesis: Heroes for Hire, Book 25
Tomas's Trials: Heroes for Hire, Book 26
Carson's Choice: Heroes for Hire, Book 27
Dante's Decision: Heroes for Hire, Book 28
Heroes for Hire, Books 1–3
Heroes for Hire, Books 4–6
Heroes for Hire, Books 7–9
Heroes for Hire, Books 10–12
Heroes for Hire, Books 13–15
Heroes for Hire, Books 16–18
Heroes for Hire, Books 19–21
Heroes for Hire, Books 22–24

About This Book

Welcome to Flynn's Firecracker, book 5 in Heroes for Hire, reconnecting readers with the unforgettable men from SEALs of Honor in a new series of action packed, page turning romantic suspense that fans have come to expect from USA TODAY Bestselling author Dale Mayer.

Some jobs are more pleasant than others...

Flynn agrees to do a security job for Levi as a trial run for more work. Looking after Anna and her animal shelter is a breeze. Trouble free. Until he leaves...

Having Flynn around was both good and bad. To have the help at the shelter was huge, but they drew sparks just being around each other. She tells herself she's relieved when he's gone but when a dead man shows up, she'd do anything to have him back.

Someone is after Flynn... and he doesn't care who he kills in the process...

Sign up to be notified of all Dale's releases here!

https://geni.us/DaleNews

Chapter 1

H E DAMN WELL better be there. Anna Burrows whipped down the road, turned into the compound and braking hard, stopped abruptly in front of the garage. Part of her was absolutely ecstatic to see Katina, while another was equally so to see Flynn. But the biggest part of her was furiously angry with him. And she planned to take a strip off his hide. If he wouldn't stand still long enough for her to do that, she would rip into him one way or the other. She hopped out and slammed her car door. Several men stood in front of the garage, and a few more came out to see what the commotion was. Then she caught sight of Flynn. She snagged his jacket from the passenger side, stormed up to him and slammed it against his broad chest.

"Did you really think I wouldn't know?" she yelled into his face. "You did this on purpose. Why? Why would you do that?"

His face split into a huge grin. And his eyes danced with joy. She knew she had made his day, but this was way too damn serious to let him walk all over her.

A joke was one thing. But this was beyond that.

She shoved her face into his surprised one. "Well, it didn't work, asshole." She turned and marched back to her car. Then she grabbed the plastic bag from the dashboard and held it up for everyone to see.

By now there had to be half a dozen men about. All of them big badass-looking dudes. But her gaze was locked on Flynn. He was the one who had made her absolutely bonkers the last few weeks. She knew she'd been nothing but a job to him, all the sadder for the type of reaction he'd gotten out of her, but even then he hadn't been able to keep it totally professional.

From the first moment he'd stepped on her property, he'd set her ire exploding into the sky. And it hadn't calmed down yet. She shoved the bag in his face. "And if this is yours, I'll call the cops again and see if it's covered in owl blood—one that was killed last night and left gutted on my back step. And, lo and behold, this bloody knife was in your goddamned jacket pocket *in my kitchen.*"

With fury riding her like she'd rarely felt before, she pulled her arm back and smacked him hard across the face.

Absolute silence filled the air.

Then she heard a gasp. "Anna?"

Katina came running. As soon as Anna saw her best friend, she burst into tears. The two women fell into each other's arms. Not one of the men said a word.

Finally, when she had calmed down enough to stop crying, Anna hugged Katina again and said, "I'm so sorry. But I had to come and tell him that I knew what he did."

Katina shook her head. "Something's wrong, sweetie. Flynn might be a lot of things, and I certainly don't know him as well as the others, but I do know the type of man he is. He'd never hurt an animal."

Anna lowered her voice and whispered so the men couldn't hear. "What about a woman? As in my heart?"

Katina pulled back to stare into her friend's eyes and must have understood as she didn't say a word, but Anna saw the question in Katina's gaze. Anna shook her head.

"I'm sorry," Katina whispered. "I was hoping things would work out better between you two." At that Katina turned and stepped in front of Anna, fisted her hands on her hips and glared at Flynn. Then she took one step forward and poked him in the chest. "If you hurt one hair on any of her animals, or on Anna herself, and let me add her heart to that list too, you will answer to me." She glared at him, almost eye to eye.

Behind her, Merk said, "Easy, Katina."

Without breaking her stare on the shocked man in front of her, she took one step back and reached out a hand. Anna grabbed it immediately. Katina wrapped her arms around her friend and said, "Come on inside. We don't need to be around him."

She shot a look at Merk that had him holding up his hands and saying, "It wasn't me."

Anna nodded her head in defiance at him too. As the two friends walked inside, Anna whispered, her voice loud enough to carry backward, "Is that Merk?"

Katina nodded.

"Well, now I understand."

FLYNN STOOD IN complete shock. He'd only returned home earlier this morning, from a quick job Levi had sent him on. He'd been looking forward to seeing Anna as soon as he could get the time.

However, this was not the homecoming he'd envisioned.

Very few things in life could shut him up. A woman's tears made him blubber apologies left, right and center, but her anger—that unjustified and unprovoked attack just now by Anna—well…he didn't have a clue what to do about it.

The other men surrounded him.

"Flynn, what the hell was that all about?" Levi asked. His tone was hard and uncompromising.

Flynn looked at Levi and said, "Shit, I'm not sure."

"Even if that knife was used on that animal, we know it wouldn't have been you wielding it. But, for the record, could you please state that?" Merk asked.

"I have never in my life intentionally hurt an animal," Flynn said, shaking his head in bewilderment. "Yes, this is my jacket. And yes, that's my knife. But I thought I lost it at her place."

Stone leaned against the garage doorway. "She mentioned calling the police once already. So I'm assuming she found your jacket with the knife in the pocket afterward."

"Right, but I didn't gut any owl." Flynn couldn't tear his gaze away from the doorway the women had disappeared into. Sure he'd left his jacket in her house on purpose. But in the kitchen. And *that* he could explain, if he ever got the chance. But he really didn't want to do it in front of all the guys. As for both his personal and professional life— although the lines had blurred many times in her case—he'd prefer to keep them as far apart as possible otherwise. Particularly as the former wasn't exactly headed the direction he wanted it to go and maybe never would now.

He ran his hands through his hair and rubbed his face. "When she calms down a bit, I'll talk to her."

"When she does, we *all* will," Levi said. "She's made this public, and made accusations. We have to get to the bottom of it."

Flynn looked at Levi and nodded. "We can do that." Inside his heart was sinking. Damn, he really wanted to be a part of this unit. He didn't need this. But it was so typical to finally make headway in his life just to have something blow up and, literally, smack him across the face. "I have no idea what she's talking about, but I had nothing to do with killing an animal."

Stone punched him on the shoulder. "We know that. We just have to convince her."

From a few steps away, Merk said, "You're also missing a very major point here. Not only did somebody have access to her house to put the knife into your jacket pocket, chances are good he knew exactly what would happen between you two by doing this. So what you need to ask yourself is, who the hell hates you enough to set you up for this?"

Flynn stared at him in shock. "No one. I made a lot of enemies in the military. Hell…" He looked around at everybody, his arms outspread. "We all did. But nothing at this level. This is…" He shook his head. "I'd never hurt an animal."

"So what happened hits you at one of the most painful levels possible?" Stone asked. "Interesting."

With a sinking heart Flynn knew he'd have to apologize, somehow convince Anna he had nothing to do with this, and then get to the bottom of it. These guys were right—somebody was pinning this on him.

"I need this sorted fast," Levi said. "We have three jobs, people." They were just setting up all the teams to head out. "With this coming down on you, Flynn, you have to stay local."

"Oh, hell no. I was so ready to go off on another job."

Levi nodded. "Understood. Depends on what we find out." He nodded toward the inside of the house. "So the sooner the better. You ready?"

Flynn felt as if he were being led to the slaughter. He took a deep breath. "Damn, yeah. I guess I shouldn't have left my jacket there."

"In her kitchen, I believe we heard her say," Merk said, one eyebrow raised.

"Not by me," Flynn said, one hand up as if swearing to God. "As much as I tried, I never quite got her there. But she has an asshole hanging around. He's trying to start a relationship, yet she's been saying no all along. He's just not listening. He saw me around the place a couple times. I figured if I left my jacket someplace—like, in her *kitchen*— then he'd believe there was more going on between us, and he'd get the hell out of her life. Honestly the guy is messed up."

"Enough to kill an owl and pin it on you?" Stone asked, turning to face him.

Flynn frowned. "Maybe. But I assumed he loved animals too. He was always talking to them." Flynn stared at the doorway again. He was a huge animal lover. He'd enjoyed helping Anna at her place. The few weeks he'd been there had been an easy job, which gave him a chance to indulge in his love of animals of all kinds. To think of somebody going in there, killing even an owl, well, that was heartbreaking. That it had been left on her doorstep was disturbing. As a threat, it said the killer could get to an animal anytime, as well as Anna. Flynn wouldn't be happy until he resolved this, as much for her as for him. The last thing he wanted was to start his career at Legendary Security with a tainted history.

He knew Katina and Anna had been best friends for a long time. He didn't want anything to get in the way of that. But he had high hopes for Anna himself. He'd met very few women who faced up to him, and who got his emotions rocking and rolling like she did. There was a whole lot more to their relationship that he was only starting to figure out. He had tried damn hard to get her into his arms and still planned for it in the near future, but he had come to realize she wasn't the one-night-stand or easy-on/easy-off type of affair. And that was a good thing as he wasn't either, but it did mean he had to slow down.

She was the type you took home to your parents and married for life.

That had set him back just enough to reconsider his own long-term plans.

When Levi had a quick second job available for him, Flynn had jumped at it, thinking distance would help him put his relationship with Anna into perspective. Only problem was, he left four days ago and was home again this morning, with her right back into his life. And from what he could see—in his heart—she'd damn near made herself a permanent home.

Too bad she didn't look interested in spending any time there, as she'd just proven.

No, he was better off alone. Damn. Even though she was a bit volatile, he had liked her all the more for it.

Chapter 2

S HE SAT INSIDE the massive kitchen beside Katina with a hot cup of coffee in her hands. She could feel her rage and pain fading. She'd needed to vent. At someone. She hoped she'd chosen the right person. She certainly was justified with the jacket mess. Only she didn't know for sure if he'd killed the owl. If he had, what was to stop him from attacking her other animals? That inherent threat scared her. These animals didn't deserve this shit. Why would anybody kill them so unmercifully? She shuddered.

Katina reached an arm around Anna's shoulders and hugged her again. "It'll be okay. Just take it easy."

Anna raised tear-stained eyes to her friend and said, "Why would anybody hurt an animal?"

Katina winced. "We know that many people would say it was only an owl, but it was so horribly…" She swallowed hard.

"It had been gutted. Essentially there's no rhyme or reason."

"Often we can do nothing about it but catch the assholes who did this and put them away."

Anna had been trying to find good homes for the animals at her shelter, but in the meantime, they had her to look after them. And maybe that was why she felt so bad. What if this guy came back? She'd never thought Flynn did this, but she'd lost it when she'd found the bloody knife. The guilt just ate at her. She was alone again since Flynn left. Permanently, just over a week ago.

It hadn't taken long for the reality to set in. He'd been a huge help getting the backlog of work done, and he also maintained a steady presence there. One she'd been happy to have. Also, the extra hands made the work go so much faster. Without him there now, all the chores fell once again on her shoulders. She'd become used to having his assistance. She wasn't sleeping well at night now either. She thought there had been an intruder the night before, but then realized it was probably just her nerves. Now she had to rethink all of this.

But she hadn't called the cops last night. She hadn't done anything because she had nothing concrete to tell them. But she'd called this morning about the gutted owl. The police came and took notes and pictures. She'd given a statement, and they'd left. She had no idea if they gave a damn. After all it was *just* an owl.

Feeling sorry for herself, she'd had a crying jag in her bedroom, and only then did she realize Flynn's jacket was on her chair. It hadn't been there earlier. It was hanging on the back of her door, and she'd smiled when she'd first seen it there—right after he had left her, his job done—knowing he'd come back for it. But she wasn't smiling now. She didn't even know how it had gotten in her bedroom because he had been gone for over a week and sure as hell hadn't spent any nights in there with her. But it was definitely his. And when she had picked it up, the knife had fallen from the pocket. One with dried blood.

Even now she couldn't quite explain to herself why she hadn't called the police again right away and shown it to them. Instead, she came racing out to the compound. And now that she was thinking straight, something even more horrific gripped her throat. If that knife had been used to kill the owl, then the asshole had been inside her house, her bedroom. And placed the jacket on her bedroom chair.

Dear God, had he been in there while she was asleep?

"Do you think whoever killed that animal was inside your house?"

Anna stared at Katina. "He had to because I found that knife inside Flynn's pocket, and the jacket was in my bedroom." She gripped Katina's hand hard. "I just don't know if he was when I was there."

She cast her mind back over the most recent time line. "The dogs were fine last night when I took them for a walk at eight, and when I went to bed at eleven, there was nothing wrong, no sign of a disturbance. But between then and six this morning, the owl was left, but the dogs didn't kick up a ruckus." She shivered. "I just can't stand the thought of somebody hurting my animals."

She lifted her coffee cup and took a sip, sniffling back the tears. When she heard loud sounds—signifying the men were coming inside—she stiffened and hugged the cup a little harder.

Katina gripped her fingers with her own. "Don't worry about the men."

Anna shot her friend a look. "How can I not?" She shook her head. "I wasn't exactly a calm, rational female when I got here."

"And you had good reason to be upset." Alfred walked over at that moment and put a plate of tarts down in front of the two women.

Katina gasped in surprise. "Alfred, these look absolutely

delicious."

"When life gets us down, sometimes we all need a treat." He disappeared with a quiet smile.

Anna watched him go. "How come all the good men are in that age bracket?"

"In Alfred's case I'd take the jump," Katina said with a laugh. "If Merk wasn't around, that is."

Anna slid her friend a sidelong glance. "You guys tying the knot again?"

"Quite possibly. He hasn't asked me officially. Afterward I'd have to answer, officially, and we would then make plans—officially." She shrugged. "We haven't gotten that far."

"I'm really happy for you. Obviously you were meant to find each other again."

"I wish I didn't have to be kidnapped or tormented like I was to make that happen."

"But you did what was right, and that's what counts."

The two women shared smiles. They'd been friends a long time. They had a damn good idea of just how rough the world could be. Especially when it came to two women alone. Anna's mother was alive—if that was what you called somebody who spent a lifetime in and out of jail. They'd parted ways when Anna was sixteen. She'd had a really rough upbringing, and maybe that accounted partly for why she would go off the handle at times. One of the biggest things that burned her ass was injustice. She was always there for the underdog. Which was how she got herself into so much trouble.

And why she helped the animal world.

The shelter was a full-time job in all ways but income. She was constantly looking for ways to increase the donations and took on other small jobs to help out. Yet it was hard to keep the money rolling in. She worked as a dog walker and did any number of other odd errands to pay the bills, but every month there seemed to be a shortfall. She had a couple companies that donated a lot of the cat and dog food. But the vet bills were getting pretty rough. She'd wondered about putting herself through school and becoming one herself just so she could look after the animals.

The men arrived and took seats on both sides of the big table. Anna glanced at Katina, who smiled brightly at everyone. Anna really hadn't had a chance to look at any of them, other than Flynn. Now she felt really bad because Levi had sent Flynn to watch over her when Katina had become a target. And instead of actually thanking him for looking after her, she'd flown off the handle at Flynn.

Always wanting to own up to her mistakes, she straightened and whispered to Katina, "Which one is Levi?"

Katina looked at her in surprise, then as if she realized Anna didn't know any of the men, set out to do introductions. One by one, when the man's name was called, they nodded their heads at her.

She realized they all looked at her a little strangely. "I'm sorry for the explosive entrance," she said. "Waking up to find the gutted owl on my doorstep and Flynn's knife in his jacket pocket in my bedroom appears to have sent me over the edge. I'm not normally this volatile, but I care about animals greatly, and it's really unnerving to think that the asshole who did this"—she couldn't help glancing over at Flynn—"had not only been in my house but in my bedroom."

Several of the men straightened as if they hadn't quite made that connection. And of course, why would they? She hadn't given them all the information. She turned to the man Katina had introduced as Levi. He was studying her with a different expression, but didn't appear to be mad, although from the look in his eyes, she wasn't exactly sure what he was feeling.

Hurriedly she said, "I never got a chance to thank you for allowing Flynn to look after me and mine while Katina was in trouble."

"And yet, as soon as we remove Flynn, you get into your own?"

She shook her head. "Well, not quite. He left, what? Seven—eight days ago? He stopped by once, but this just happened last night."

Silence reigned as the men looked at each other. Levi nodded. "But if somebody had been watching the place, they would know you were no longer around. So if you were out of the picture, why put the knife in your pocket to firmly put you back into the picture?"

Silence.

One of the other men, a monster of a tank, leaned over the table and asked Anna, "Did you tell the police about the knife?"

She shook her head. "No. They came this morning and spent a short time there. When they left, I went into my bedroom, and that's when I saw the jacket."

"And you didn't call them again?"

She shook her head. "No, but I should have. For some reason I came racing here instead." She made a funny face. "Like I said, I don't normally fly off the handle like this."

An odd snort came out of Flynn's mouth.

She glared at him. "Although some people do seem to prick my temper a little more than most."

One of the men on the other side of the table, she thought his name was Rhodes, spoke then. "Flynn's like that. He does it to more than you, believe me."

"Hey, that's not fair." Flynn laid his hands on the table. "I didn't do anything."

"But somebody went to a lot of trouble to make it look like you did," Levi said. "We need to know why. And if it's connected to anything else."

"To anything else?" Flynn asked. "What do you mean?"

"You were looking after Anna because of Katina's kidnapping case. It's possible that whoever is implicating you now could be a part of that case in some way."

Katina straightened beside Anna. "Oh, please, don't say that. I thought for sure we got everybody."

"And given the time frame, chances are we have. However, that doesn't mean it isn't connected to something else. Not only did Flynn leave your place, he then hooked up with Logan."

Levi turned to stare at a different man, leaning against the kitchen wall, one Anna hadn't seen before.

"Logan has been attached to several of our cases, so it's possible Anna and her shelter were just caught in the crosswinds of something much bigger, deeper, and uglier."

Levi turned to study Anna.

She gave him a small smile. Her only thought was *holy shit*. She didn't know this man, but he seemed to be searching her, studying her, like he knew something she didn't. It was a daunting feeling.

Just as she was about to nervously ask Levi what was the matter, one of the most strikingly beautiful women she'd ever seen walked into the room. Levi lit up. The woman sat beside him, smiling directly at Anna, and said, "Hi, I'm Ice."

"Hi, pleased to meet you."

Obviously Ice and Levi were partners. There was just something about the way they sat together, not to mention they were perfectly matched, like a tight couple. Fascinated, Anna watched as they appeared to have a low conversation, almost in code as they finished each other's sentences.

Finally, Levi turned back to Anna. "As much as we hate to dig into your personal life, we have to ask a few questions."

She straightened and frowned at him. "What does that have to do with this?"

"Is there anybody who hates you enough to do something like this? Any neighbors who hate the fact you have the shelter and maybe want to shut you down? Do you know anybody who would be angry enough at Flynn for being in your life that he might find this an avenue to turn you away from him?"

Her jaw dropped. Slowly, she pulled herself together. She considered the questions for several moments. "I've never heard any official complaints, but I know several of my neighbors weren't too happy with my animal shelter. I do have a large piece of land on the outskirts of the city, and most of the properties there are almost as large, so there's distance between us. I get a lot of traffic through my place, but it would be hard for my neighbors to have any grounds for complaint as it's not steady.

"I don't think we ever truly realize who might hate us or just dislike us. As far as I know, there's nobody with a grudge against me. I haven't had any major breakups, put anybody in jail, nor had arguments with anybody to that extent. So that shouldn't be a concern. As for anybody who'd be angry at Flynn being there, well, it only makes sense that I would have somebody around the place to help out. I have in the past. Flynn was only there for a few weeks." She frowned at Levi. "I'm not sure what you're getting at."

From the far side of the table Flynn said, "He's asking about past boyfriends who might think I was somebody you were hanging out with."

She sent him a frown. "As you well know, I don't have a boyfriend, so it's not an issue."

"And what about Jonas?"

"What about him?" she snapped. "We only met for coffee once at the mall, then he started hanging around the place because he's lonely. I don't think he has many friends, but we didn't have a relationship."

"He's not taking no for an answer," Flynn reminded her. "I sent him away that day, remember?"

She stared at him for a moment, and then her confusion cleared. "Sure, but that was only one time. He was just trying to see me. You know he comes around now and then. I figured he was harmless. Whatever mood you were in, you didn't want to let him in."

"Well, maybe it was because he was high. He was completely stoned out of his mind and shouldn't have been there."

She shrugged. "That's not unusual apparently. He's like that most of the time he's been around the house."

"He was also very angry at seeing me there."

"Well, you were inside my house."

Silence.

She slumped back into her chair. "He was upset because he saw you inside my house and figured you were my new boyfriend." She looked at the men at the table. "So now you're all considering it was Jonas who killed the owl, and placed a knife in Flynn's jacket pocket to incriminate him, so I'd be angry?"

She looked around at all the faces and added, "Right, of course. But that wouldn't work as I do know who Flynn is inside." She dropped her head in her hands. "If I hadn't been so upset and scared, I wouldn't have said what I did in the first place."

Glumly, she stared at Flynn. "For the record, I don't believe you had anything to do with killing that owl. I saw you work around my animals. You're just not that kind of a guy." She stared down at the table. "Now I feel like an idiot."

Katina, still sitting beside her, said, "No, it was fear. And coming here was right. You came here to get help. Whoever it was thought they'd set Flynn up and got the opposite reaction to what they expected. The good thing is, they don't know about it."

Anna turned to frown at Katina. "I don't get it."

"They might have thought you'd fly down here and break it off with Flynn. But instead you came to be safe, and get help. So instead of breaking up with Flynn, all you've done is get his attention to help solve this for you." Katina smiled. "The opposite reaction. But still the right thing for you to do."

Feeling like a fool and wishing she could just leave now, Anna muttered, "It doesn't feel like it."

Just then Alfred arrived bearing platters of big sandwiches and wraps cut in pretty little pieces.

Hurriedly, Anna stood up and pushed her chair back. "I'm so sorry. I didn't mean to intrude on your luncheon."

Katina stood up beside her. "Don't worry about it. You're welcome here."

"No, that's not necessary."

The two wrangled back and forth until Flynn stood up and roared, "Sit down."

Silence. Again.

Anna glared at him. "You're not in my house on Levi's orders, so you don't get to boss me around any longer."

In a low deadly voice, he leaned across the table, his large hands flat on the surface, and snapped, "Sit down, damn it, or I'm coming over there and making you."

"Don't you dare threaten me," she growled right back, leaning over, her hands near his on the table, shoving her face in his. "Just you try it."

Then she heard it. A snicker. Then a choked laugh. And suddenly the entire group at the table erupted in laughter.

Mortified, she sat back down and buried her face in Katina's shoulder. Arms came around her, and she realized her best friend was laughing too.

Such was her day.

AS THE LAUGHTER broke out, Flynn sat down with a hard bump. How nice that he and Anna had provided entertainment for the crew. It wasn't exactly how he wanted to introduce them to her. She really was special. He had hoped that having a break from each other would make her seem less so in his eyes. New attractions were always deadly. He wanted some time away to ensure what they had was potential enough to go after.

Her accusations had stunned him. Her apology just now only slightly less so. He glared down into his coffee cup, wondering how long it would take for this hilarity to die down.

When the laughter finally stilled, Levi spoke up. "First thing is to get the knife to the police. Should be simple enough to test it to determine if it was used."

Logan, sitting opposite Katina at the table, said to Levi, "We can test that here, you know."

Levi tilted his head at Logan.

"It's really simple to determine certain things about blood," Logan said. "But our sampling must be small so the police can have the rest for whatever tests they have to do." He nodded toward Anna. "If you want to come with me after lunch, we can see what our testing kit can find."

"Thank you," she said in a neutral tone.

Flynn studied her downcast head. This had been a tough morning for her. He couldn't imagine the shock of finding the bloody knife in his jacket pocket. He knew it was his, just as he did that he'd lost it; therefore, he hadn't been the one to bloody it. Not this most recent time at least. It may have some on the blade, but it could be human, and it would be a degraded sample—something from a long time ago during one of the more ugly missions he'd been a part of in the Middle East. He'd cleaned his knife, but the best labs could always find evidence—and they would find something.

Still, it was bothersome. He hated to think of her all alone in that place with a madman running around killing animals. It was a very small step from that to humans, as he knew all too well. Nothing like being in the military— particularly when he'd been over in Afghanistan and Iraq— to shake his belief in humanity.

The atrocities he'd seen had been shocking. He had no problem with animals being killed for food, but he hated to see them starved, abused, injured, or toyed with. It was one of the reasons he'd been so happy to help Anna. It gave him a chance to reconnect with the animal world he'd missed so much.

And for that he was grateful.

Stone, who had been quiet up until now, asked, "Any chance the man who did this was either the previous owner or neighbor?"

Anna frowned at him. "It's possible, but I don't know why now though."

"But it is a line to tug," Flynn said. Not that he had the time. He was supposed to be heading out of town. At least he'd really been hoping to, but according to Levi that wouldn't happen now.

"First things first, let me take a look at the blood on the knife." Logan glanced over at Flynn. "You still have it?"

Flynn pulled the bag out of his pocket and handed it over.

Logan stood up and said, "With any luck I've got five minutes to set up my tests before you guys eat everything. The actual results take longer." He turned and disappeared out the door they had come in.

Stone stood up, picked up his cup of coffee, refilled it at the sidebar and followed Logan.

Flynn watched as several of the women got up and went to the kitchen to help Alfred bring out the rest of lunch.

The others stayed seated at the table and talked about opening a lab in the compound, but they needed the money set aside for it before doing so. Expansions were expensive, and all kinds of equipment were needed. Apparently, a morgue quickly became a hot topic as well. From what he'd heard about the attacks on the compound so far, he conceded that would be a need. Though a large walk-in freezer would be a better option.

After lunch, several people headed back to whatever they were doing before the interruption.

The place was large, and well over a dozen people were in and out on a regular basis. He was one of the newest and still finding his own place. Having Anna storm in this morning had just added to his problems. But he was more concerned about her.

Katina still sat very close to Anna, their heads huddled together as they talked. He wondered what it was like to have a friend like that.

Guys had buddies. They hunted, fixed cars, and barbecued together with a case of beer open beside them as they talked about everything, but nothing personal. These two women shared such a special bond. And he wondered how that worked for them.

He got up, refilled his coffee and sat back down across from Anna. When he noticed hers was empty, he winced, stood again and poured a cup for her.

She raised her eyes to him. "Thank you."

"Just relax," he said. "We'll get to the bottom of this."

Logan came back in, his face grim and his voice hard. "I heard you say that." He shook his head. "But it's a whole lot more serious than that."

Levi came in from the kitchen. "What did you find?"

"The blood in the bag and on the knife is not animal. It's human."

Anna gasped, her hand covering her mouth.

He held up the bag containing the knife for everyone to see. "And it's covered from one end to the other."

Flynn's stomach knotted. He turned to Anna's pale features.

Logan continued, "I don't suppose you found a dead

body—other than the owl—on your property, did you?"

She shook her head, saying, "No."

"Did you even look?" Flynn asked.

"Why would I?" she cried. "I found the owl and was so upset, it never occurred to me to keep looking. And then I found the knife in the jacket. Obviously I assumed you used it on the owl."

Flynn looked to Levi. "Definitely past time to call the cops."

Levi nodded. "You'll need to take her to the station and hand over the knife and jacket."

He nodded as he stood up, looking at Anna. "Are you ready?"

"For what?"

"I'm taking you to the cops in Houston." He glanced at the others. "And then I'll go back to her place to see if we can find a body."

She let out a hoarse cry.

"You want company?" Logan asked. "I got nothing better to do today, and I would like to see how this goes."

Flynn nodded.

He and Logan had been buddies for a long time. He wouldn't mind having him come along. Something was seriously off, and he knew better than most how important it was to have someone he trusted to watch his back.

Chapter 3

ANNA HUDDLED INSIDE her jacket. She was grateful she'd thought to grab one. She couldn't believe the sudden turn of events, and was really not looking forward to a trip to the police station. Then somehow going home with Flynn on one side and Logan the other was completely the opposite of what she thought would happen this morning.

To find out the knife was covered in human blood changed everything. She cast her mind to what she thought she'd heard last night and everything she'd seen this morning, but there had been nothing to indicate an injured human was anywhere around. She just couldn't believe this.

They made the trip in complete silence. As they entered the city, Flynn turned to look at Logan and asked, "How about a change of plan? We should check on her place first, make sure there isn't something else to find, and then report to the police."

"Good idea," Logan said. "We'd look pretty stupid if we take a knife in, then go to her place and find a body."

She shrunk down into the seat a little farther. The last thing she wanted was to find anything else dead around her place. At least she had a decent security system. But what good was it when an intruder could shut it down, like this one must have? The cost of running the place was so high she was barely limping along. She had several acres here in what had been the outskirts of Houston, only the city had grown up around her—increasing her taxes and utilities. How could she set up security for the entire place? It would cost a small fortune.

Flynn drove into the driveway and parked off to the side. Stuck in the middle, she had to wait for the men to get out first. She hopped down, walked up to the front door to unlock it, only to find the door was ajar.

"Shit."

"Shit what?" Flynn stepped up and seeing the door open, pushed her out of the way and pulled a weapon from his back pocket.

She'd almost forgotten about the fact he carried. Sure this was Texas, and she should be used to it, but there was something about the way he wielded it. He was a man who knew exactly what to do with that weapon. And wasn't scared of doing what needed to be done.

It wasn't comforting before, but now it was downright soothing.

Both men had their weapons out and walked into her house quietly. "Stay here," Flynn whispered.

She made a face. She wasn't stupid. She would let them go first, but no way would they keep her out for long. She was terrified of what might happen to her animals in the back.

After giving them a long moment, she peered around the corner into the front hallway and living room. It seemed normal. As upset as she had been when she left earlier, there was a chance she forgot to shut the door.

She walked in and followed the men as they searched the entire downstairs. She shrugged. Nothing appeared to be wrong or out of place. "Maybe I forgot to lock up," she said.

She walked to the kitchen's back door. It was closed, the lock in place. She opened it and went toward the animals in their kennels. With her heart pounding, she walked through the shelter, checking all the cages, finding everyone safe and sound.

She turned to face the men and realized only Logan was here with her. "Where's Flynn?"

"He's gone to check the rest of the house."

That made sense. "All the animals are here and accounted for."

She walked to where the dogs were kept. She hated to leave them for very long. As soon as she got home, she would move them out to the yard for a few hours to get some exercise.

There was Jimbo, a big golden Lab, and Duggy, a pitbull/Doberman cross that needed freedom more than the others. She also had two small dogs, which was a blessing. She quickly shuffled the bigger ones and their pens, letting the animals out back, and they jumped and played with each other. She smiled. It was one of the reasons she did this, and a way she could find homes for them.

She took the remaining dogs and moved them to one of the smaller pens. She had four cats in residence right now. She shifted them as well. Something she normally would've done this morning.

The playhouse was in a separate room where the cats could sprawl out for most of the day. After finding the owl this morning, she'd put everyone back in their cages. Maybe a foolish thought, but now they could return to the play area.

It took a good ten minutes to shuffle everyone around. Several other animals were at her place right now, and one was a huge bunny named Bugs. But he lived outside in a pen—as long as the weather was warm enough for him. She checked and found him nibbling on grass.

That left the snake, in a glass terrarium for now, safely sequestered from the hamster in a large cage off to the side. He was snoozing in the sawdust. Happy.

"Good. Everyone here is fine," she said to herself. She turned to find Logan, standing guard. She winced. "Are you actually playing bodyguard?"

He gave her a flat stare. "Until we figure out what the hell's going on, yes. You won't be alone until then. And there's nothing playful about this."

She nodded and brushed past him. "I'm heading back to the house then."

"Wait. How much of this is your property, and is there somewhere else we should look for a body?"

She froze. "I have four acres here," she said. "You want to check everywhere? Just stay out of the dog pen. They don't know you. Other than that, do what you want."

Flynn spoke from behind her. "What about the food shed?"

She turned to stare at him. "What about it?"

"Have you been inside it this morning?"

She shook her head. "No. I don't need to. I have dog food inside."

"Then Logan'll stay with you in the house, and I'll check the rest of the property."

He glanced at Logan, and she saw as they exchanged looks.

She threw up her hands. "Fine, we'll go together." She led the way to the back and opened the double doors. "I get a lot of food donated by companies. I keep most of it in the shed."

"Is it locked?" Logan asked.

"Yes," she said. "I have to. I can't afford to have any of it go missing. It's expensive enough to keep this place up."

"You need better security here," Flynn said from behind her.

Immediately her back stiffened. "So you said, more than once." She took several steps toward the shed, adding, "As I said before, there isn't any money to upgrade."

At the shed she stopped and stared at the busted lock. "Ah, hell. It's been broken into." She'd just die if all the food was gone. There was over a year's supply stored in there. She wouldn't be able to replace it.

Her shoulders were grabbed roughly, and she was jerked back several feet. "We'll go in. You stay out of the way."

She shot Flynn a fulminating glare, but he wasn't looking her way. Instead, he and Logan were communicating in a way that was all too easy to understand. As she watched, Flynn gave a nod to Logan to open up the door.

With her gut wrenching in fear, she waited, her arms across her chest as she chewed on her bottom lip. This was one of the easiest, most accessible places on the property.

And she hadn't really considered it that way before.

Logan pulled open the door, and both men jumped in, weapons out.

When would this nightmare end? When Flynn had stayed at her place to keep an eye on her, all she'd been able to think about was the day he'd finally leave. He'd been such an irritant in so many damn ways. Yet, he'd also been fun, bringing a lot of laughter to her world. When he did leave, all she could think about was an excuse to see him again.

But today hadn't gone the way she'd hoped. She'd just been so angry and upset that she hadn't been able to think straight. Now he was here, coming to her rescue yet again, and all she wanted was for him stay.

"Anna?"

She was startled back to the present and walked a few feet forward to peer into the darkened room. "What?"

Flynn's voice was somber and hard. "We found what we were looking for."

She couldn't see anything with the two men standing in front of her. She pushed her way in between them. The shed wasn't that big. On the floor between the full racks of pet food lay a man, collapsed on the floor.

FLYNN WATCHED HER face, seeing the shock as emotions swept over her. She clapped her hands over her mouth, and tears filled her eyes. He had a sinking feeling in his stomach. "You know him?"

She raised her gaze to him. "You do too."

He pulled out his keys with a small flashlight at the end and turned it on. Focusing on the man's face. "Hell, that's Jonas, the asshole that's always after you. The damn stalker."

"Whoa," said Logan. "Her stalker ends up dead on her property. And the knife likely used to kill him ends up in your jacket pocket in her bedroom." He shook his head. "This is not good. Someone is pinning this murder on you, buddy. Who the hell did you piss off so bad they want to lock you up for twenty years?"

"No one. Hell, I haven't pissed anyone off lately. Not so they'd do something like this," Flynn protested.

"Except me," Anna muttered. Flynn gave her a sharp look, and she had the grace to look ashamed. "Okay, you have a tendency to rub people the wrong way. But that's no reason to set you up for murder." She turned to look around the small room. "What really concerns me at the moment is, to set you up, what other evidence is here adding weight to that?"

"No idea. But I didn't do it, so it doesn't matter what the hell they find. It just means I have to clear myself."

Logan said, "Hey, buddy. I know that's how it's supposed to work, but too often the cops just look at the surface. They get easy evidence, and that's it. Slam dunk. You're locked away as a murderer."

Flynn glared at him. He crouched beside the body. "He looks like he's been shot."

"Except his arm is cut up pretty bad too," Logan said, pointing to the dried blood on the dead man's sleeve.

Flynn exchanged a hard glance with Logan. "I have an ugly suspicion as to what knife might have caused that injury too. It would explain the human blood on it."

Logan held up his hands. "I know you wouldn't do something like this. We'll help any way we can. This is bullshit. I know it. You know it. But we still have to call the cops."

"I'll do it," Anna said, pulling out her phone. "It needs to be me."

Flynn pulled out his. "Do it," he barked at Anna. "I'm calling Levi."

Logan held up his phone. "Good idea. I'm calling my father. I think we might need everyone in on this deal."

Chapter 4

ANNA STARED AT the officer standing in her kitchen. "I'm sorry. Did you just say I need to leave? I don't have any place to take the animals. This is a shelter. They are here because they require someone to care for them in the first place."

"It's now a crime scene. You can't be here."

"No," she protested. "The shed is a crime scene. That has nothing to do with the animal shelter or my house."

"And yet, we think it's related to the owl being killed. The knife was found in your bedroom in a jacket pocket. Therefore, evidence is tracked to the house."

"You don't understand. I have no place to go." She stood and looked out the window at the animals. "And there are no other shelters around that can take them. That's the reason they're here."

The police officer walked several steps away and pulled out his phone. She didn't know who he was calling, and didn't care. Somebody needed to solve this. How long would her place be a crime scene? Surely a day was enough for them to get whatever evidence they needed.

If they left the animals, she could come back and feed them. Maybe she could stay somewhere for the night. She just didn't know. Often the police wouldn't let people back into their homes for days, if not weeks. That couldn't happen here. It was her home. Surely something could be done.

So far Logan and Flynn stood quietly at her side. They answered all the questions they'd been asked, but hadn't offered anything extra. She understood how Flynn felt. At the moment she was feeling pretty damn antagonistic toward the police herself.

Then she remembered that Jonas's mother was alive. That was one thing about Jonas always coming around and making a nuisance of himself—he'd talked. A lot. She knew how hard this news would be for his mother. Nobody should lose a child. Now that he was dead, she was sorry for not having treated him nicer. But he'd become difficult, a pain in the ass, someone who wouldn't take no for an answer.

But she had never wanted him dead, just to go away and leave her alone.

She deliberately kept her gaze from zeroing in on his body, instead looking at the back window of the shed. She couldn't help worrying that she might need access to the food stored there. Damn, what was wrong with her? Someone had been killed in there, and all she could worry about was the animals.

That was typical. The donation money had slowed to a trickle, and she was in dire straits. The last thing she needed was something like this. It was hard to get support for the animals at any time. If anybody thought a murder investigation was going on at the shelter, the money would completely stop.

Morose, she sat at her kitchen table, drinking coffee, waiting for the police to go through whatever it was they needed to. There was no point in fighting it. She'd given them access to the entire property. She wanted them to do their job.

The officer came back and told her, "We need the property for twenty-four hours. When it's time for you to work with the animals, an officer will be with you at all times. You can't stay here overnight, but during the day, you can be here for the animals. After that time, we should be done, and you can have the place back." He stood and waited for a response.

What choice did she have? This was the best she could get. She gave a curt nod. "I will be here from seven in the morning to seven at night. At that point, I will leave." He frowned, and she shook her head. "There are dogs to feed and walk, cats to look after, as well as cages to empty and disinfect. There's food to sort and medicine to give out. There are phone calls to make, etc. This is a business, and it's a charity. I need people to understand it's still operational."

He turned and walked away. She sank back into her chair. "That went well."

Flynn spoke from behind her. "Where are you going overnight?"

"I want to sleep in the cages with the animals," she muttered. "I don't really want to leave them alone."

"The police won't let you do that."

She propped her elbows on the table and dropped her chin into her hands. "Of course they won't. That would be too easy. I have no idea what I'll do. How's that for an answer?"

She stared out the window, wondering what the hell happened, and how she would get past this—then chastised herself for being selfish. She knew Flynn was in bigger trouble. Yet he had people backing him. People he could trust to find out what was going on and make sure this didn't have a long-lasting impact on his life. She was in the same boat Katina had been in before, and now understood why she was with Merk at the compound.

In fact, it wasn't that far away, but still she wouldn't impose on her friend any more than she had to. Mentally she went through a list of people she knew, wondering if anybody would be generous enough to offer their couch for the night. But the list was short, and the answers were no by the time she got to the end of it. No way could she justify staying at a hotel. She needed money for her own electricity, phone, and water bill. She would not blow that kind of money on a hotel.

So maybe she would have to spend the night in her car.

Logan appeared at her side. "Levi said you're welcome back at the compound until the police are finished in your house."

She turned to stare up at him. "Why would he even offer?"

Logan laughed. "He is a very generous soul. You're also friends with Katina. And obviously you have some kind of an oddball relationship with Flynn. Love and murder, perhaps?" His tone was teasing, yet with the threat of darkness and all that had already happened ...

She winced. "The murder, yes, but the love ... I don't think so."

"Hey, how do you know? Give it—me—a chance," Flynn said, his wicked grin flashing.

She shot him a look and laughed. "Flynn, you've probably left a wrecking-ball-size pathway of broken hearts in your life. I have no intention of becoming part of that."

Logan laughed. "Flynn's all talk but very little action."

"Hey, that's not true. All the girls love a hero."

At that Logan really laughed. "Don't let Levi hear you say that. He's got this thing about that term."

Flynn frowned at him. "What? Hero?"

"Yeah, that one. Ice made a joke about Heroes for Hire being the company name. And the subsequent women who have joined us at the compound have come up with versions of their own to go along with it—much to Levi's disgust."

Flynn laughed. "Oh, my gosh, that's rich. And it's actually a very good name."

"Levi doesn't think so."

Flynn grinned. "No, Legendary Security is way better than that. But as a nickname, it's perfect."

"That would make you a hero," Anna said.

"We tried that once, remember? Didn't work out so well. And you don't have the money to hire anybody, so there is no Hero for Hire here."

She got up and walked to the teakettle, filled it and put it on to heat. Inside, her mind was churning options.

The last thing she wanted to do was go to the compound. But there would be a hot meal and place to sleep overnight. She just loathed the thought of leaving the animals behind. She stared out at the dog runs. "I can't leave the animals alone. What if somebody comes back to kill them?"

"Didn't the police say they would be here overnight?"

She shook her head. "I don't believe that's what they meant. I think they just wanted to have access overnight, not that they'd be here or have guards on duty, keeping an eye on the place. I doubt they have money for that. Nor do I have it to hire somebody to look after the animals or stay in a hotel."

"You won't be. You'll be staying with us," Flynn said.

"And if I don't want to?"

"Then it would mean the two of us having a very un-comfortable night here."

"You'd stay with me?"

"Yes, but I can tell you that because it's a murder scene, the police will be back and forth searching the entire house looking for fingerprints, so the animals will be safe tonight."

She hated to be persuaded, but also knew she needed sleep. "Can I come back early in the morning?"

"Yes."

She checked her watch. It was already after seven. "It'll take me at least an hour to finish with the animals tonight."

"We can help too," Flynn said. "I'd like to be on the road in an hour."

She blew the hair out of her face. "Well, we'd better get busy then."

She started with the dogs, the two men beside her. They walked all of them at the same time for a good half hour. That cut the time way down for her. She struggled to take that many dogs at once, particularly when Jimbo, the big Lab, was rambunctious and tended to tie up all the leashes. Flynn took Jimbo on his own; she took the little ones, and Logan took the pit bull, Duggy.

Thirty minutes later they came back, putting the dogs into their cages for the night. With help, she fed and watered them, gave each a good cuddle, and then turned to the cats. She studied them inside the playhouse and said, "I can leave them all in here. We'll move the litter boxes, food, and water in there too, and they'll be fine."

They did everything needed for the cats, then she turned her attention to the outside pens with the hamster, rabbit, and snake. The hamster needed clean bedding, fresh water, and food, as did the bunny. The snake, well hidden in his habitat, always scared her when he revealed himself. She tossed some live crickets into his terrarium and slammed the lid shut.

By the time they were done, the police were still all over the place, now under outside lights. It gave an eerie look to everything.

She walked back to the officer she'd spoken to earlier. "We'll be leaving now. Please keep an eye on the animals for us."

He nodded. "They'll be fine. We still have hours ahead of us here. It's doubtful anybody else will come back tonight. If they do, they'll get a bit of a surprise."

"Let's hope they do, and you guys catch them. I won't sleep well knowing somebody put a dead man in my shed. Or killed an owl as a twisted message."

"Where exactly was the owl?"

She pointed to the back step. "It was dismembered and left on the step."

"What dogs are here now?"

"The two big guys are in the back. Normally the two little ones are in the front, but I have them closer to the bigger dogs now. Although in the front they'd notice everything from birds to intruders." She winced. "So maybe it's safer for them to be in the front."

"They'll be fine. See you in the morning then."

With the two men at her side, she was persuaded to head back to the vehicles. She was taking her car; she wanted full autonomy to leave in the morning. Otherwise there was a good chance Flynn would stop her.

She got into the driver's side, and as she put the keys in the ignition, Flynn slipped into the passenger seat beside her.

"You can ride with Logan, you know? I'm perfectly safe."

"But I want to ride with you," he said. "Besides, I need to explain something."

She shot him a shuttered look as she pulled out onto the street. Logan was ahead of them. She planned to follow him right back to the compound. She worried that Levi hadn't been given an option about her staying there. It may be that Flynn had somehow pressured Levi into letting her come back. She'd made quite a scene this morning. She wasn't sure she was even welcome.

"Explain what?" The truck ahead of her took several turns and then turned onto the highway. She followed him, and within seconds they were heading down the main road toward the compound. It wasn't a very long drive, but it was one she didn't remember well.

"My jacket."

"Was it?" She looked over at him in surprise. "I thought you were explaining something about the compound."

"As much as I love being part of that place, it's impossible to explain," he said with a laugh. "I'm still figuring out exactly how it all works."

"You sure I'm welcome?"

"It was Levi's idea."

She shrugged. She needed to be happy with that, though she wasn't. She still felt like he had been pressured into it. "What about your jacket?"

"I left it on purpose."

"What the hell did you do that for?" She stared at him in shock.

"Two reasons. One, if Jonas came into your house—your bedroom—he would see it and realize you are in a relationship, and maybe leave you alone."

"Jonas doesn't go into my bedroom. Never even went into my house." Then remembering Jonas lay dead in her shed, she added, "And obviously it's way too late to worry about something like that now." She still didn't quite understand Flynn's meaning. "What do you care if Jonas thought I was in a relationship?"

"Jonas was damn creepy. Any woman should have been terrified of him."

"Well, now that he's dead, I don't think it's an issue."

"At the time I didn't realize his demise would happen quite so fast. And I was more concerned about you."

"Well, thank you for that, but it was completely unnecessary."

There was an odd, uncomfortable silence, and then she remembered he said he had two reasons. "What was the other?"

When he didn't answer, she studied his profile as he stared out the passenger window. "Well?"

FLYNN NEVER BEAT around the bush. He was a straight shooter. He prided himself on that. And when he first opened his mouth, it was with the full intention of telling her more about his jacket. But it just felt odd now. The timing sucked. And he was really big on that too. It seemed like lately everything he did was out of sync with what he should've been doing.

The best time of his life was when he had been an active SEAL. But even then, the timing had sucked. He'd been in Afghanistan, and his orders at the time would've been completely normal and fine, if he had been in the right place. But he'd lagged behind, and gone into a village to help somebody on their way back when nobody would help them. He'd stayed longer than he should. When he had explained it to his CO, he'd been reprimanded. When the orders came through that they were pulling out, and he needed to leave those children in trouble, it went against his better nature, and in his ire, he disobeyed direct orders.

His famous Irish ire. That damn temper of his got him in more trouble. He ignored the orders to return to camp. Instead he helped set a broken leg and then assisted the injured mother with carrying the children back where they would be safe. By the time he made it to camp again, he was in deep shit.

If there was ever a black day he remembered, it was that, and no one wanted to hear his side. It didn't matter that he was doing a good thing. He did not follow orders. The other guys didn't sympathize. In fact, several of them got really angry.

But his CO was an asshole. It didn't matter how good a job you did sometimes anyway. So Flynn had spent a year traveling, "finding" himself. It didn't all suck. It was a great year, but the thought that he'd been having a midlife crisis already at thirty wasn't something he was proud of. But he was lost. Angry, disbelieving the sudden turn of events, and it had taken a long time to get back on his feet.

But now he had a shot with Levi's company, and didn't want to lose it. This was what he was geared to do. Born to do. They were all former SEALs. He knew that would change over time. A lot of other really good men were out there who he knew would like a chance to join. But Legendary Security was a fledgling company, and Levi could hire only so many people at one time. Yet his company was growing. Flynn had no doubt in a few years, this would be *the* company, and he wanted in now.

So when Levi had asked Flynn to look after Anna, the answer had been an instant yes. He'd jumped at the chance and would have done it for nothing, like his official job interview for Levi, so Flynn had been delighted when he was paid.

But nothing had prepared him for meeting Anna. Or for the attraction. It wasn't all one-sided either. He lived large. And he loved well but was looking for something so much more. In Anna, he'd found it. Only they'd argued—a lot. And he'd loved every minute of it. When he'd been told by Levi it was time to pack it in, Flynn had been disappointed but accepted that the job had come to an end. When it came time to actually go, he'd had a hard time leaving things the way they had. So he had left his jacket behind on purpose.

"Are you going to tell me?" she asked. "Is it some deep dark secret you don't want anybody to know? What? Have you been holding a candle for me?" She sneered. "I know that's not true."

He glanced at her. "I guess I deserved that."

She frowned and stared at him.

And he knew she didn't understand. "Because I did leave the jacket behind for a specific reason. It gave me an excuse to come back and see you." He gave a heavy sigh. "And maybe I was staking a claim. So that if any man went inside, he'd see it and know my clothes were there first."

Her gaze widened, and she jerked her attention back to the road. She didn't say anything for a long moment. He slunk back into his seat prepared to sit in silence until they got to the compound.

"And why did you want to come back and see me? All we did was fight."

"Not quite," he said quietly. "Or have you forgotten the kiss?"

"I haven't forgotten *anything*," she mumbled.

He grinned at her emphasis on *anything*. Maybe this wasn't as much of a lost cause as he was afraid it was. He certainly hadn't misunderstood her response to their passionate kiss, but it was something they hadn't gotten a chance to talk about, until now. Leaving the jacket behind was his way of saying, *I'm coming back*. Apparently, she got the message.

As they entered the compound, she slowed and came to a stop in the middle of the road. She looked over at him and said, "Where should I park?"

He pointed at a spot between two of the company trucks. She pulled up and shut off the engine. "It feels weird to be back so soon."

"It shouldn't. It should feel just about right." He gave her a warm grin and exited the car.

As she got out, she turned and asked, "Do you think it's related to that night the dogs went crazy?"

He frowned.

"You know that night …"

He realized several of the men in the garage had turned at their arrival. Of course she chose this moment to bring up what should have been a private conversation.

He thought back to the night in question, realizing he didn't remember much about it, but there had been a ton of barking outside. "You're thinking there was an intruder then?"

She shrugged. "I don't know. It just was an anomaly, and now something else has happened, so I have to wonder."

"What was an anomaly?" Levi asked, approaching.

Flynn winced. Great. Now Levi would think Anna was better at this job than he was. But no way in hell was Flynn walking into a new company, a new job, lying about something. "The night before I left her place, we heard something. It wasn't very much, but it set off the dogs. We didn't find anything at the time though." He glanced at Anna and added, "She's wondering if someone had been checking her place out even then. But what for?"

He motioned her to enter into the garage, and from there he'd take her into the kitchen and find her a spare bedroom. "Now with the killing of the owl, well, that only makes me more concerned. The only reason to do that is to terrorize her."

Levi nodded. His gaze was assessing as he watched Anna walk into the kitchen, and Alfred took over from there. Flynn and Logan remained in the garage, knowing Levi had more questions.

"Do you think she's hiding anything?"

His question was directed at both Flynn and Logan. The two men looked at each other.

Flynn said, "I don't think so. I worked with her for a couple weeks. What you see is what you get. She has a temper, loves to argue. She's passionate about the animals. But I don't think she's deceptive. I never saw any instance where she was lying, and she doesn't use feminine wiles to get her way—she's direct." He shrugged. "I think she's very honest. And she's just horribly upset and shocked by what's happened."

"And I'd have to agree, from the little bit I've seen of her," Logan said. "She's had a particularly tough day. The cops are all over the place. The animals are upset. And, of course, she knew the dead person."

"How well?" Levi turned to face Flynn.

"Not well. They met accidentally the first time, and she was nice to him. He started coming around all the time after that. Being more of a nuisance than anything. She felt sorry for him." He opened his arms. "You know how that goes. He kept coming around, hoping she'd change her mind."

"Was he violent?"

Flynn shook his head. "He never laid a hand on her. He seemed to always be high, coming on or going off from his look. He was fixated on her, obsessed, and if he hadn't died, I'm sure he would have become a much bigger problem. How big of one, I can't tell you."

"We've already done a search on him. Nothing we found changes that. He didn't have a steady job or relationship, but had money. He didn't own property. The vehicle was in his name, but his mother was paying for the insurance. He's done time for small crimes, like petty theft, possession charges, and some breaking and entering, but all on a lower scale."

"So he got himself killed?"

"Or else," Logan said, "he was in the wrong place at the wrong time."

Levi pivoted to look at Logan, then said, "And if we look at that hypothesis, why was he there in the first place? Who needed to take him out because of it? What was the killer doing there?"

Flynn shook his head. "I have no idea."

"How many people knew you were there, Flynn?"

Flynn stopped and looked at the ceiling, contemplating how many actually knew where he had been at that time. "You and your team, Logan's dad, anybody he might have told, Anna, and me. We didn't get out much, just staying on her property. I don't really have friends or family who care. And I wasn't there long enough to make an issue out of it."

"Because what we really have to know here is, why you were set up. Was it to throw deflection from the killer? Or were you the target and Jonas incidental?"

Flynn stared at him as he finally understood. "There aren't too many people who'd go to that kind of effort to set me up."

"How many?" Stone asked from behind him.

Flynn spun, not having heard the big man creep up. Flynn shook his head. "Damn, you're silent."

Stone studied him. "Don't deflect from the question."

"It's just not a pleasant time in my life."

"All the more reason we need to know about it in case it's related."

"Back when I was a SEAL, I went rogue and was booted. I'd do it again in a heartbeat. But at the same time I was kicked out, so was somebody else. He wasn't with me, but he blamed me. I have no idea what reasoning or evidence the military had for their actions toward him."

He stood stiff, not knowing if any of them were aware of the circumstances surrounding him leaving the military. If they were, he hoped they'd understand his position.

"What was the man's name?" Logan asked. "I don't think you told me about that, buddy."

He glanced over at Logan. "Nobody likes to smear dirt. Especially not with a fellow SEAL."

"His name?" prompted Levi.

Flynn considered his options. Then shrugged. "Brendan McAllister."

Instantly, the other men stiffened and nodded knowing-ly.

"You already know him, I presume?"

"We know him, and you're right," Levi said. "It's not nice to say anything bad about anybody. But if we were, it would be him. He was a lazy lowlife, and he would never have had your back. He was a coward through and through."

Harsh words for a SEAL, for anybody in the military, because if there was one thing everybody needed, that was to know your teammates had your back.

"I heard he was dishonorably discharged," Stone said. "Good thing. I'd have kicked him across the country if they'd given me half a chance."

On that note, Flynn turned to head to the kitchen. Several of the other men joined him.

"I'll get Dad to look into that," Logan said. "He knows his brother. But no two siblings could be as different."

Levi asked Flynn, "Any idea if Brendan is local?"

Flynn stopped. "I don't know."

Logan grabbed his phone. "I'll find out."

"I thought he lived in California," Flynn said. "But that may not have been his choice after he was booted." He pointed toward the kitchen, then said, "I need to show Anna where she will be staying."

"Alfred's got that well in hand."

Of course he did. What would they do without Alfred? Flynn walked into the kitchen to find it was empty. That was also when he realized he'd missed dinner. With any luck some leftovers were in the fridge. He opened the huge double-door appliance, checking to see if he could warm up anything.

As he turned around, Alfred walked into the kitchen, heading for the dishwasher. He pulled out two plates. "I'll have your meals ready in a minute."

"I think Logan's probably hungry too."

Alfred laughed. "Okay, make that three plates." He reached inside the big metal dishwasher and pulled out a third one.

"Anna is in the room beside yours. You'll probably have to bring her back down, otherwise she will not eat. She looks like the kind who doesn't want to impose."

"You got that right."

Flynn was happy to be the errand boy in this instance. He was also delighted that Anna had been put in the bedroom beside his. Alfred was very astute. Maybe he saw something there. Flynn hoped so. But it was way too early to tell.

Chapter 5

THE NEXT MORNING Anna woke up early. It was almost six o'clock. She had a quick shower, got dressed and then made up the bed. With a last glance around the place to see if she left anything behind, she grabbed her bag and walked down to the kitchen. If she was lucky, coffee might be on; if not, she would slip out and head home. The animals needed her.

At the kitchen she stopped to see several people up already. "Wow, I thought I was the only early riser."

With a light grin shining in his eyes, Flynn stood up. "I heard you moving around and figured you'd be sneaking out early."

She glared at him. "I wasn't sneaking anywhere."

"Good, because Alfred's cooking breakfast."

She smiled in delight. "I wish I could steal Alfred away from you."

"Not happening," Levi said, "and you're certainly not the first to try."

She sat down on the far side of the table, watching as everyone came in the room in various states of wakefulness.

When Katina came in and saw her, she dashed over to give her a big hug. "I'm so sorry I didn't see you when you got in last night. I was really tired."

Anna studied her friend. She caught sight of a blush

across her cheeks. She'd let her friend get away with the white lie. If Anna had been sleeping with someone like Merk, she might've had a reason to go to bed early too. She winked at her friend and watched the pink deepen on her cheeks.

Katina smiled. "I was thinking about coming to your place for the day. Maybe I can help out. If nothing else, I can keep you company. It's got to be lonely as hell there."

"We can spend a few hours there, but that'll be all," Merk said quietly. But there was no doubt he meant what he said, and he wasn't budging on the time line.

Katina looked at him and frowned. "Why?"

"Going to Gunner's place. He has information he wants to discuss in regard to Flynn, Logan, and another man named Brendan."

Katina hadn't heard the other news last night.

Neither had Anna. After it was quickly explained to her about this Brendan, she frowned at Flynn. "Why didn't you tell me?"

He raised his eyebrow. "Why would I? That was a long time ago. It's a dead issue."

"Apparently not." She turned to Logan. "And your father confirmed that Brendan is living locally?"

Logan nodded. "Supposedly he's staying with his brother right now."

She dropped her gaze to her coffee cup. "As much as I'm happy he might be a suspect in this killing, it is also kind of unnerving that somebody would hate Flynn so much to kill somebody else." She took a sip of her coffee and added, "How does any of that make sense?"

"We don't have any answers at the moment," Flynn said calmly. "But what you will find is when we do, it will make more sense. Maybe not in the way you would understand, but to the killer, it always makes sense. That's one of the few sad things about people who kill. In their own twisted way, they have a good reason for doing what they do."

"Scary thought." After that, the conversation went to general topics. She watched as platters of sausages, bacon, and eggs came to the table. "Alfred, how can you possibly feed this many people all the time?"

He laughed. "I love it. The bigger this place gets, the happier I'll be." And on that note he turned and walked out.

She raised an eyebrow at Levi. "How big are you planning on making this place?"

"No idea yet," he said cheerfully. "We have lots of room to expand. Depends on the work and need for our services."

She nodded. "It's still empty without animals though."

He laughed. "You're not the first to mention that. Personally, I think all the women want me to bring in a bunch of dogs and cats."

"Well, if that's the case, I do have a few that need homes," she said brightly. "Just let me know, and I'll deliver them personally."

He shook his head. "No way are we going there yet. It would have the workmen in all kinds of chaos around this place."

Flynn raised his head. "Workmen? What's happening next?"

"We're reworking a couple apartments and planning to build a lab. Ice seems to think we need some kind of morgue."

Anna gasped, her gaze zooming toward Ice. "You're kidding, right?"

"Not really. But it could be a cold room for keeping

foodstuffs as well."

"All the health authorities would love that," Anna said with a laugh. "And those guys aren't easy to keep happy at any time."

"Have any of the regulatory bodies made life difficult for you?" Ice asked. "I mean, when we talk about having enemies, very few people actually consider institutions, like health authorities, coming in and closing them down."

"I'm sure groups like that are on some people's list," she said with a smirk. "But no, I haven't had any trouble with anybody."

"Interesting that the best suspect is actually somebody who went to your place as your bodyguard," Levi noted.

Anna glanced at Flynn and quickly said, "That doesn't make him responsible."

"I'm not for bringing him there," Flynn said. "But I might be for pissing him off enough that he wanted some payback."

She leaned forward. "And how does killing Jonas give him that?"

Into the silence that suddenly filled the room, Flynn said, "If I get charged with murder, one I didn't commit, that's a hell of a payback."

"But to kill a man?" She shook her head. "I just don't get that. But I don't live in the same world you guys do. Killing is very alien to me. I'm in a world of saving lives, even if they're mostly four-legged furry ones."

She glanced at her watch and said, "And speaking of which, I need to get going." She stood up and grabbed her dishes, walking into the kitchen. Alfred was there, loading the dishwasher. "Let me rinse these first."

He turned, saw the dishes and smiled. "I'll handle it, my

dear. You take that basket there. It's got lunch and some coffee for you, as well as a few muffins just in case you get hungry. You don't know what kind of mess your kitchen will be in," he rushed to add. "Remember the police were there, and they tore your house apart all day. It could be very upsetting for you when you get home."

"I was trying hard not to think about that." She gave him a sad smile. "It's just work. I can clean it up. I hope the animals survived the night without too much stress. The last thing they need is any more upset."

She walked back into the dining room and picked up her overnight bag she'd dropped in the hallway. She turned to Levi and Ice. "Thank you so much for giving me a place for the night. I need to go and check on the animals."

To the chorus of good-byes, she waved at everybody and headed back through the garage out to her car.

And found Flynn standing at the passenger side.

"What are you doing?"

"I'm going with you," he said calmly. "You have no idea what you're going into when you get home. You shouldn't be alone."

She frowned, realizing she really didn't want to be, but it wasn't good to leave him stuck there. "Don't you want to have your own wheels so you can come home again tonight?"

"You forget several of the guys are going to Gunner's place. I can always catch a ride home with them."

Her face cleared of worry. "I had forgotten. I get to see Katina for a few hours today too." On that much happier note, she got into the car, turned on the engine and waited for him to get in and buckle up, then she pulled out of the compound.

DAMN, HE THOUGHT they'd gotten well past that point. But it seemed like she really didn't want him around. Or at least not at night, and that made no sense, considering there had been an intruder at her place, inside as well. He had no intention of leaving her alone in that house, not until this was resolved. The fact that somebody was after him could possibly mean he was putting her in danger. But why didn't this guy face him? There was nothing worse than having an asshole sneaking behind your back, causing mayhem and murder.

He'd had enough trouble living with it in the military as it was. He was sent on missions to ferret out these assholes one by one. But it wasn't something you expected when you hit home ground. And he'd been out of the military now for almost two years.

But apparently, he'd also lost his edge. And that would be a concern. If not to him, then to Levi. If they didn't think they could trust him, then they wouldn't assign him to help out on missions. The others had to know he was there to watch their back. And he had been watching hers.

As the asshole had gone inside her house after Flynn had left, had the killer been watching her place? Had he known Flynn had left? For good? Or had he expected Flynn to be there to take the hit instead of Jonas?

The drive was smooth and fast. When they pulled into the front driveway, cop cars were still parked there. He could almost sense the waves of relief coming off of Anna, presuming the cops had been here since yesterday, so nobody else would have shown up through the night.

He got out, leaving his stuff in the backseat. She hadn't noticed he'd brought an overnight bag, and at the moment, that was fine with him.

He reached the front door ahead of her, found it un-locked and walked in. Nobody was inside. He turned back to her and said, "I suggest we talk to the cops first."

She nodded. "Works for me."

But instead he went to the kennels. Of course she pitched in. Very quickly they had all four dogs moved to the outside pens. After scratches, cuddles, and boisterous good mornings, they turned their attention to the cops and walked around the feed shed.

Flynn watched one man, standing on the far corner, tak-ing pictures of the entire property. He pointed him out to Anna. "Two cop cars are outside the house. There should be at least another man around."

With a heavy sigh she said, "It's a big property. He must be here somewhere, digging into things he shouldn't, most likely."

"There you are."

Flynn turned to see the second cop coming out of the shed. "Good morning."

The cop nodded. "We're almost done here. But while we're working, we don't want you wandering around the property disturbing things."

Beside him, Anna huffed with annoyance. Flynn stepped in before she could say something. "We came to look after the animals. We'll try not to disturb you."

The cop nodded. "We appreciate your cooperation."

"I presume I can go inside and get clothes, etc.?" Anna asked.

The officer nodded. "The house is fine now. That's not where the killing took place."

"Where was he killed?" Flynn asked.

The officers studied them quietly for a long moment and

then said, "Out back of the shed."

Anna slipped her hand into Flynn's. He squeezed her fingers reassuringly and asked, "Was he stabbed?"

"Don't have an autopsy report, but it looks like it from our initial viewing." The officer stepped back and said, "Of course you realize I'm not allowed to discuss anything else in the case." He gave a curt nod and walked back to the shed.

"What could he possibly be doing after all this time in the shed?" Anna asked as they turned away. "Hopefully we won't need to grab any dog food out of there today."

"I filled up all the bins before I left."

"Good. They won't steal any, will they?"

He laughed. "I don't think that's an issue. But grabbing anything with forensic evidence, like blood, they would. On the other hand, they only want the packaging, not the dog food in it."

She shrugged philosophically. "Okay, let's take care of the animals."

Flynn was surprised at how easy it was to fall back into the same routine he'd had for several weeks. They moved down the aisles, cleaning cages, watering, feeding, and changing dishes. Thankfully, there actually weren't many animals.

Then he remembered the cats. As he walked over to the big playhouse, they were all in various states of snoozing. He loved that about cats. The rest of the world could go to hell in a handbasket and they would just lie there and say, *Yeah? And what's it got to do with me?*

The litter boxes, however, was a pretty major deal. They had three in that one room alone. All had to be changed out every morning. He took care of that as Anna filled the food bowls with a mix of wet food and brewer's yeast in some kind of a broth. He knew nutrients were added to it, and apparently the cats didn't mind.

At the sound of Anna and him coming into the room, they all woke up. They twisted around his legs and acted like they hadn't eaten for at least a month. He knew better. This was their daily routine.

He picked up a ginger-colored tom and gave him a hug and pat. The cat bumped his forehead against Flynn's chin over and over again, but his motor was running like a Mack truck. No doubt the cat had kind of stolen Flynn's heart. But no way was he set up to have pets. He gave the cat a kiss, walked him over to the food and dropped him down beside the dish where there was an open space. The diesel engine noise never stopped. But the cat dove in and started eating.

With that done, he followed Anna back into the house. They stopped and surveyed the kitchen. Things were just shuffled about, but there didn't appear to be anything missing. She had a ton of clutter around as it was. And a lot of it had to do with the animals—leashes, collars, and all kinds of doggie and treat bags.

He walked to the coffeemaker and checked to see if she had coffee in the cupboard. Seeing several packs, he opened up the coffeemaker, placed a filter in it, added water, then coffee, and put the glass pot under it to catch the drips. He didn't know how long they would be here, but he assumed he had enough time to drink a pot.

As he turned to see what she was doing, he found her sorting through a stack of mail on the table. "Is that today's?"

She shook her head. "No, these are bills that have been stacking up for a while. They hit the third and final notice before I pay attention."

He winced at that. "That's got to put a lot of stress on

your shoulders."

"Yes, but it's the only way I survive. If anybody gets their money early, then somebody else has to do without, and those really get nasty."

It also explained why there was rarely any food in the fridge, the cupboards were damned near bare, and why she was not so much skinny as borderline scrawny. There had to be a way to get more money to help out at the shelter so she could keep some food on the table for herself.

He studied her clothing. They seemed to have seen years of wear, and even her shoes were cracked with her socks peeking through the front outside seams. He knew she was prideful, but she really needed help. He just wasn't sure he had anything to offer. He wasn't wealthy, and his bank account sure proved it.

But he did know lots of people. There had to be a way to get some interest in this place. Or she would have to disband and find another way to make a living.

Then he realized this wasn't her way to make money. For that, she did all kinds of other jobs. But everything she earned went into keeping this place running for the animals, and all the charitable donations went toward the center.

Shit. With all the cops here, donations would be nonexistent from now on.

She picked up an envelope with no return address and frowned. She quickly ripped it open and out popped a check. She gasped, and sat down in a kitchen chair, hard.

"What's the matter?" He strode across the kitchen floor to study her. She held it up so he could see. It was a bank check for $10,000.

Chapter 6

H ER MIND GRAPPLED with the concept of a big influx of cash like this. The number of bills she could pay off, the needed repairs she could make to the shelters, food she could actually buy for her charges—to supplement the free things she received–and the medicine she needed for the animals ...

Suspicion ran through her mind, and it was a hard thing to let go of. She took a closer look at the check and said, "I don't know who Goldberg Holdings is."

"Does that matter?" he asked. "It's a hell of a nice check."

She nodded. "It's marked 'donation.' I'll send him a receipt right away."

"It would be more prudent to see it clears the bank first," he said in a dry tone.

She laughed. "Isn't that the truth?" She set the check off to one side, excitement still thrumming through her at all the things she could fix. There would even be enough money left to leave in the bank for future needs for other animals coming to her small shelter. As she tossed bills to one side, she found another envelope. But this time it just had her name and address on it. She pulled it out and asked, "What the hell is this?"

He looked at it and said, "No idea."

He held out his hand, and she dropped the envelope into it. There was something about it she didn't want anything to do with. "I only want it if more money's inside for the shelter."

He gave her an odd look and opened it. There was something small inside. He dumped it into his hand and gasped.

She glanced up at his face to see it had suddenly hardened. "What is it?"

"A SEAL insignia," he said. He laid it on the table with the envelope, brought out his phone and took a picture.

She figured he would send it to Levi. "But why would somebody send that to me?"

"I suspect it was intended for me." He put the phone down and studied the small metal piece. "There's nothing on it that I can see though."

"Why would there be? Are you expecting the sender to sign it?"

He shot her a look. "Wouldn't that be nice?" He looked at the stamp on the envelope. "It was mailed from Houston."

"But it has my name on it. Not yours."

"True enough, but the one man we think could be involved was a SEAL also. As far as I know, he's living somewhere local."

And she realized she'd been really slow to get it. "Of course, you think it's a warning from your friend."

"Not so much that as a statement...*I'm here.*"

She sighed. "You know? It would be really nice if you would take your macho bullshit far away from here."

"It's too late for that. A dead man was in your shed, or have you forgotten?"

Her temper snapped as she said, "Of course not, but that

owl was left as a message for me."

"I'm sorry." He sat back and rubbed a hand through his hair. "I didn't mean to snap at you. It's not your fault."

"Glad you remembered that." She bounced off the chair and walked to the coffeepot, pouring two cups. She brought them back and set them on the table.

"Have you gone through the rest of the mail? Let's make sure nothing else is there before I make a few phone calls."

"There are still some letters in the stack." She shuffled through them. "Electricity, water, insurance, flyer, flyer, flyer, garbage. That's it."

Flynn picked up his phone again and started making calls.

As Anna went back through the mail, she opened the bills, stacking them off to the side. For the first time in ages, they wouldn't cause quite the same pain they had before. Ten thousand dollars would do a hell of a lot of good here. Several of the bills were duplicate notices. She stapled those together within the pile, then picked up the rest of the junk mail and tossed it into the recycling bin.

When he was done on the phone, she turned to him. "Will you tell the police?"

He glanced at her, already dialing somebody else. "What would I say?"

She chewed on her lip as she stared at the metal lapel pin. "I don't know. There's just something…evil about it." She didn't want it in the house. But then she didn't want any of this. "Did you tell them anything about who you suspect is involved?"

Instantly, he shook his head. "No way. I don't have any proof. And if he didn't have anything to do with it, I don't want to ruin his life a second time by sending the police sniffing around his place."

She slunk back down in her chair and tugged her coffee closer. "I guess that makes sense. But it really sucks. What a mess."

"Maybe. Focus on your good morning already. That check helps cover some of the gloom from this insignia."

She stood up again. "On that note, I can go to the office and take a look at where the money will be going. I really needed this check. So thank you very much to whoever Goldberg Holdings is."

She grabbed the bills and her coffee cup, and strode to her office in the back of the house. She didn't know if the cops had been through her whole house or even in her office, searching through her finances or what. If they had, they would have seen a sad sight. Whatever. She somehow suspected they had the right to do what they needed to. With a dead body being found on her property, what else could she say but *help yourself to any information you need.*

She didn't even have a chance to grieve for Jonas. Not that she knew or liked him very much, but he was somebody who had died, whose life had been unexpectedly cut short. And for that, she was very sad. That it happened on her place was horrific.

She added this newest stack of bills to the existing pile and set to cleaning up her office. Nothing like finally having money to clear the debts to completely change her perspective on the business. She went through the stacks of paperwork on top of the big desk and decided to reorder her bookshelves to make space for all the stuff. She quickly set about organizing on a deeper level. By the time she was done, she was ready for her second cup of coffee.

She returned to the kitchen, refilled her cup and went

back to the office. Flynn was still on the phone. Good. Her hands were full with shelter problems.

Anna brought up her Excel sheets and tallied the money she owed. She could do a general expense transfer for some of them and quick payments of other bills online. That would mean a trip to the bank first to make sure the check cleared. But it was the safest route. She didn't have enough to cover all these bills if that check bounced.

She hopped to her feet and walked into the kitchen. "I'm running to the bank to deposit this."

He looked up at her. "Good idea, but you're not going alone. I'll come with you."

"I want to go now, straight there and back. I want to pay off all the bills."

He smiled. "And you look excited about something for the first time."

"Yeah, no kidding."

She grabbed her keys and walked out the front door, Flynn right behind her.

The trip to the bank was fast and efficient. The teller assured her the check had cleared already; they'd checked the sender's bank account, and it was all good. Anna turned around and gave Flynn a huge smile. "In that case, let's buy a few groceries."

He laughed. "We'll do that later. Let's go home, take care of the rest of the stuff that needs to be dealt with, like the police. Then we can shop."

She nodded.

As they walked back into the house, a cop stood in the middle of the kitchen, looking for her. He frowned and said, "Where the hell were you?"

She stepped back at his sharp tone. "I had to deposit a

check in the bank and pay some bills."

That seemed to mollify him. "You need to take a look at something in the shed."

"Fine, let's go."

The three of them trooped out to the shed. Thankfully, the body was long gone. Blood remained on the floor and a couple feed sacks. She worried she'd never get the stain completely out. Even so, her memories would still be there.

The cop pointed out something at the back wall of the shed. "Is that yours?"

She walked toward the rear and saw an old rifle leaning against the far corner. She frowned. "I don't own any guns. And to my knowledge that was never here." She turned to look at Flynn. "Have you seen it before?"

Flynn approached, studied it and shook his head. "No, I don't recall seeing it here either."

"You two sure?"

She nodded yes and turned to the cop. "You should remember if it was here last night. Nobody mentioned it?"

"No, it was hidden under old coats and blankets," the officer said. "It was missed on the first inspection."

She backed away and said, "I presume you are taking it with you."

He nodded. "We will to test it."

"Whatever you need to do to solve this is fine with me." She turned and walked out.

If she could replace the shed with a better storage system, she would do it immediately. She would never be inside it without thinking of Jonas.

"I'M OFF TO finish this paperwork."

He watched as she headed into the office. He'd seen her office many times. Stacks of unpaid bills and receipts were all over the place. She was doing too much on her own, as usual. He followed behind, stopping at the doorway, amazed at how much she had already cleaned up. Nothing like an influx of cash to change your attitude. He would have to thank Goldberg Holdings for the help.

She might be offended if she knew it was Logan's father. On the other hand, she didn't have any reason to know. Gunner had lots of money. And he was big on helping charities. If he had known beforehand that she needed it, he would have gladly helped. He was a big animal lover. So was Logan.

Flynn's phone rang. He glanced down and saw it was Levi. *Finally.* "What's up?" He turned away from Anna's office and headed to the kitchen.

"According to Gunner, Brendan is living at his brother's place, has no job, but is applying. He appears to be diligently establishing a new life. He was really angry but has since calmed down."

"So we're not thinking he's the guy? I'd still like to know where the hell he was these last couple weeks. Anywhere in Houston is certainly close enough to be on alert."

"Understood. Have you found anything else in the house that'll point to him?"

"No, but the cops just found an old rifle in the back of the shed where the body was." He quickly explained the little bit he knew. "It's a little too obvious, considering it hadn't been there before. If someone wants to pin it on me, they'd have to have my fingerprints on the stock."

"Which is not hard to do, as you well know."

His voice turned hard and abrupt. "I know." He stared

out the window for a long moment. "This is really unreasonable though. I mean that's a long time to hold a grudge if it's him."

"But you were pretty damn angry yourself about what happened and how it went down. He's much more volatile. If he still hasn't let go of his anger, I can see him taking time to find a way to pay you back. Maybe he had no idea where to find you and just happened to see you in town. That could have changed things for him."

"It would explain why he was really angry, then disappeared and got angry again. Revenge is best served cold."

"It so is. Watch your back," Levi said.

"Yeah, will do. Levi ..." He hesitated. Maybe he didn't want to know the answer to the next question. But it was hard not to wonder and worry if this would end his career with Legendary Security.

"What's up?"

"Will this stop you from hiring me?"

"I already hired you, remember? As far as I'm concerned, this hasn't changed my mind, but we need to put this to rest to free you up so we can send you on missions. There's enough work here for half a dozen more men. I just don't need the baggage that comes along with this case." And Levi hung up.

That was good enough for Flynn.

Whistling, he focused his attention on the kitchen. Quickly cleaning up the mess the cops made, he worked on the rest of the house. When he'd been here before as a bodyguard for Anna, it had been difficult to keep busy, to ignore his cravings for Anna's presence. She became one of those addictive kind of personalities. He knew what she would say, how to get a rise out of her, and when he got that expected response, it would cause some fireworks.

She was fully passionate in everything she set her mind to, which immediately sent him to consider what she'd be like in bed. One kiss was not a seduction. But it was a hell of a start. Now there was much more to consider. Not just how or when to further this relationship, he also couldn't let whoever was trying to ruin her life get a second chance. Her safety had to be paramount. Anybody who killed one defenseless guy already probably wouldn't hold back on killing a woman. And Flynn intended that that would never happen.

Chapter 7

I T TOOK SEVERAL hours, but by the time she was done, she felt so damn relieved and happy it was hard to express. She paid off the very last bill, jotted down the confirmation number on the back of the deposit slip, clipped it together with the bills, and filed them away. She shut down her computer, got up and danced around her office. She was free and clear. She poured every penny of her paychecks into this place, and finally she had some money to help cover things.

It was amazing. The bills were taken care of with just under $1,000. How was it that little of an amount could make such a damned difference? But it had. Now that she had caught up, she could hire someone to fix some of the cage doors. All kinds of little bits and pieces of things needed to be done. She had to find a decent tradesman to help out.

She did have someone in mind, but she should also call the vet and see how much she owed for all the work he'd been doing. Charity was helpful, but people couldn't do it forever. At some point people appreciated getting paid.

She sat back down again, twisted her chair so she could stare out at the huge yard behind her house and kicked her legs up to rest on the windowsill.

Anna sat there for a long moment. For the first time in a long while, she felt peace and contentment. It had been a hard road getting here. And she certainly owed Goldberg

Holdings a huge thank you that she was back on top again, hopefully at least for a full year. She'd probably lost her dog-walking business with the madness of the last couple days.

And maybe this was a crossroad in her life.

She didn't know.

Plus, other shelters were always looking for a place to move animals to. She was a no-kill center, but most in Texas killed thousands of animals daily, all combined. It broke her heart.

So many humans and animals ended up in need because not enough people gave a damn. And for those who did, everybody had their favorite charities. And so many good ones existed and were deserving of the donations, but so was her small shelter. She was competing for dollars among bigger nonprofits. It was hard to get the attention she needed.

Maybe she could look at marketing again, like posting an online ad. Even just having someone hug the animals to let them know they weren't totally alone would be great, which she could accomplish with a visit to a local nursing home or senior center. And that would help the humans there too. On better days she used to take the dogs and cats around to various pet supply stores on weekends. Many of the animals were adopted that way. But there were just so many and the need so great that it often didn't work out.

She hated taking the animals back to their cages. They needed so much more than that lonely space. But at least they were safe while she found homes for them. And they had dog runs and company here.

Yet what she was doing here was barely enough.

"That's a pretty long face for somebody who just got ten thousand dollars."

She jolted at his voice to find Flynn leaning against the doorjamb with a cup of coffee in his hand, staring at her. "Decisions, decisions," she said. "Never easy ones."

"The money wasn't enough to cover what you needed it to?"

"Oh, it is. For the moment it's huge, but I have to think long-term what I should do," she said. "Limping along like this is not a good answer. I could stay and continue as I am. Hopefully better than I've been doing so far."

"With money or time?"

"Both." She stood up and walked toward him. "Are the police still here?"

He nodded. "But it looks like they're packing up."

"Great." She smiled as she glanced around the office. "Things can go back to normal."

"Whatever that means, considering what has happened."

She took a deep breath. "I'm also wondering about selling the property and moving the shelter."

"Why would you do that?" His tone was anything but happy.

"Well, the murder for one," she exclaimed. "How many people do you think will donate money after this?"

"But somebody just did."

"No, the check was sent before this happened. Chances are there won't be more to come." She turned to stare out the window. "It's a large property, and real estate prices have gone way up as the city grew around me. I could sell."

"And do what?"

Her shoulders fell. "Of course that's the problem, because I don't really know what else to do. This is where my heart is."

"Then wait and see. You don't have to decide today—or

this week or month. You have time. This will blow over. And eventually things will return to normal."

She twisted to look at his face. Then asked that one question sitting in the back of her mind. "Do you think he's done?"

Flynn didn't pretend to misunderstand. "There's no way to know. Unfortunately."

"You're thinking this might be related to a previous problem you had in the military."

"Maybe. But no way to know that either," he said simply.

She nodded. "Isn't it ironic Levi sent you to help because of a problem with Katina, and you bring yours here instead?"

There was silence, for longer than she intended. Her gaze intensified. "I'm not blaming you."

"I'm blaming myself." He turned on his heel and stepped back into the kitchen.

Yeah, that wasn't her finest moment. Of course he would take it that way. Maybe she'd intended for him to. Push him away a bit more. But she really didn't like what was happening to her shelter. Although this work was where her heart lay, she wasn't so sure this place was where her future was.

She turned and stared out at the animals, realizing that before when she'd been upset and disgruntled, finding her world tilted, the animals had put her back into balance. And she needed to do what she did best. She went down to spend some time with them.

"NO, I HAVEN'T said anything to her," Flynn told Levi, walking over to the far side of the living room and staring out the front window. The cops loaded the rest of their gear into their cars. Good that they were done. Not so that they were leaving. A police presence was a great deterrent.

"Make it look like you're leaving. If there'll be another attack, we suspect it'll be while she's alone."

Flynn agreed with that. It meant he'd have to stay inside away from the windows and prying eyes. "She might still kick up her heels over it."

"It doesn't matter if she does. She's not safe. I put you there, and we brought this problem to her door. We have to fix this."

"Does Gunner have any insights?"

"Lots. He's tracking down Brendan. But so far his brother doesn't know where he's been today—or yesterday."

"Right." Flynn frowned. "It's pretty damn thin motivation to think he's coming for me after all this time."

"I know." There was a harder note in Levi's tone. "Are you sure you told us everything about your involvement in Brendan leaving the military?"

"I didn't have anything to do with him leaving. I was kicked out because of not following the orders I was given. Brendan was over there at the same time, but I don't know what happened."

"Was he with you?"

"I'm not exactly sure how it all played out. Brendan passed me a message to bring me back to base. I refused because I was busy helping the villagers. I have no idea what Brendan said to the CO. At the time, Brendan had a lot of hard feelings because he felt I got him kicked out. I knew I did myself, and was good with that. But I did talk to the CO and explained that Brendan had nothing to do with me disobeying orders. I don't know why he was kicked out."

"Right. Maybe I can ask someone about that." Levi's voice trailed off. "I have a mission I need you on. Now I'm wondering if maybe it will be safer to send the two of you so Anna gets out of there for a while."

"And the animals?"

"Logan said he'd be happy to step in to stay there and look after them."

"And what if he's attacked instead?"

"Logan would be prepared. He wouldn't come alone, and he's military trained. Like we all are." At Flynn's lack of response, he added, "I know. I'm just tossing out ideas here. Looking for the best way forward."

"That's for Brendan to face me."

"A great idea. But it's not going to happen. As he's already demonstrated."

"One thing I do wonder though," Flynn asked, "is why Jonas was here?" He shifted position to make sure Anna wasn't listening. "I understand he was probably at the wrong place at the wrong time. But what was his reason for actually being here in the first place? And was there something behind the killer picking him? I'd seen Jonas twice the entire time I was here, but Anna said she didn't see him that day at all. What was he doing at nighttime on her property?"

"Do you think he would break in?"

"I have no idea what he was trying to do, or might've thought. I do understand that he was after Anna. But she hadn't given him any kind of encouragement, so if he was here for... The neighbors have a security camera, but Anna's was out."

Levi's tone turned businesslike. "East or west?"

Flynn chuckled. "I can't guarantee that it shows any-thing."

"But we can't discount it until we've seen it."

After the phone call, Flynn walked outside around the house, to see just what the security feed might have seen. It was pointed at the space between the two properties. But given the angle, it might very well show activity going on in the back of her house. The animal shelters were in the center, while the dog runs were horizontal on the sides. But the shed could possibly be in the viewing angle.

Walking back toward the kitchen, his phone rang. Levi calling him back.

"The police say they've seen it, and nothing was there."

"I was just out checking the angle."

"Stone's actually patching us through. I'll get back to you in a few minutes."

Flynn walked into the kitchen and once again checked the fridge and all the empty cupboards. He went into the office and found Anna gone. From the window, he saw her in the backyard, working with the animals. As he watched, the dogs jumped and scampered as she threw balls and picked up sticks, generally cuddled and played with them. This should be a full-time job for her. No question. But he understood her concerns about staying here.

He wondered if a quiet conversation with Gunner would make any difference. Logan had already gone around Anna as it was. Was the shelter something they could actually help with over the long-term?

What she needed was a couple major benefactors to keep the animal shelter flourishing. Plus, to find more places to give these animals homes. And it could take a while. If a few people would support the place, it would go a long way to add some validity to the shelter. All he had to do was tell a few friends, who'd tell a few more, who'd then tell more. He mentally wrote it on his To Do list. He'd spent a fair bit of time in Logan's home with his family, knew about their love for animals and extensive network among family, friends, neighbors, and businessmen. He'd start there.

Texas had a huge animal problem, and if Anna could do her bit to help out, then he wanted to assist her. Everyone should have lofty goals.

His was to become a valuable member of Levi's company. And to do what he loved. Although he was here, he had a tenuous relationship at best with Legendary Security. Not exactly the start to a great working relationship he'd hoped for. On the other hand, Levi had stepped up in a big way.

And that just made Flynn appreciate him all the more.

Flynn turned his attention back to Anna and decided it was time they went out for a meal. Then they could go shopping for food. He walked outside, headed toward her.

Just as he entered the pen, he heard a sound he'd never forgotten. He threw himself at Anna and dropped them both to the ground.

Chapter 8

"**W**HAT THE HELL?" Anna rolled onto her back, the dogs all around them barking and yipping. The two little ones tried to clean her face. She wasn't exactly sure what just happened, but Flynn was busy dragging her behind the side of the shed. The dogs followed, jumping, thinking this was a great game. She stared at him in confusion. "What was that all about?"

"I think somebody shot at us," he said in a harsh whisper. "A sniper."

She stared at him in shock. "Who does that? Who lives like that?"

He gave her a wry look and said, "I did. We all did. None of us are looking to do it again now."

She watched as he quickly placed a call. She wondered if anybody else had noticed that sound. She'd heard a boom, but it was kind of a low one. For all she knew a branch had snapped off a tree or something. How he had recognized a silent sniper shot said much about his history.

She didn't understand why someone shot at them, but while Flynn talked to Levi, she had to get all the dogs to safety. Probably moot now. If somebody had actually fired that first shot to kill, chances were very good they could've taken out any of the dogs easily enough. It also bothered her that she now hid behind the shed where Jonas had been found.

Was it the same killer? And how the hell would she get out of the middle of this? Not only did it not have anything to do with her, but somebody had now made it her fight. And that was a whole different story.

"Will do." Flynn turned to look at her. "That was Levi. They're still running the feed on the neighbor's house, looking to find something."

"I doubt they'll see very much."

He nodded and peered around the shed. "If there's any chance of you staying here at all, consider upgrading your system. I can get this one up and running, but you'll need way more than you've got."

"*I* need? You mean, *you* do. This asshole's after you."

"But he targeted your place. Your animals. Your friend."

She winced. "Hardly a friend but okay, I hadn't really looked at it that way."

"And you should. We are in this together now."

"We were from the beginning," she muttered. "How the hell will I ever get my life back?"

He leaned over, studied her face for a moment, then reached down, snagged her chin, lifted it, and kissed her. "We will figure this out. This too will pass. In the meantime, we have to catch the asshole. Then we will make your place bigger and better. Wherever you choose it to be."

She stared at him in wonder. That was kiss number two. Nowhere near as exciting as the first, but the words behind it were so much more reassuring. She waited for something else to happen outside. The silence around them crackled. No birds chirped; not even the dogs barked. In fact, they all lay down beside her, staring at her as if to ask *What's happening?*

Knowing it wasn't the right time, but because of that

kiss, she couldn't resist. "Does that mean you're staying?"

"Yes." That brilliant gaze turned toward her, studied her face, and he smiled.

Not quite the answer she was looking for. But what had she expected? A declaration that he couldn't stay away or something else out of a romance novel? Not likely. She had to remain grounded. "How long until you fix the security?"

"I'll have it done before bedtime."

She knew he was searching every inch of the place, looking for the shooter. But he didn't have binoculars. "Why was the old rifle in the shed?" she wondered out loud. "It really doesn't make any sense."

"So much in life doesn't. The chances are good he managed to get my prints off something and put it on the rifle."

"So that gun is what killed Jonas?"

"That's what I would've done if I was pinning the murder on somebody else. Of course it's a little too neat—placing the murder weapon in the shed where the victim was found. You want it to look like it's been hidden but not so hard that the police can't find it. But that wasn't even a good effort."

"It's a little scary to hear you talk like that."

"Don't worry about it. I never killed anybody who didn't need it." He shifted suddenly and raced around the far side of the shed, calling back in a loud whisper, "Don't move."

She pulled her knees up to her chest and wrapped her arms around them, getting into as small a ball as she could. She was hardly well-hidden. She was alongside the shed where the fence line was. But she was certainly open on that side. One of the dogs crept closer and whimpered. She wrapped her arms around him and pulled him on her lap.

The least she could do was make him feel better.

She thought she had a family for these two small dogs—an older couple whose children had left home, leaving them as empty-nesters. It'd been on her To Do list to call and see if they were still interested. Both dogs were in good health and young, with a lot of happy years ahead of them. They shouldn't be in a war zone, like she was currently living in. As soon as she got back to the house, she vowed to call them.

She glanced at the two bigger dogs. They were definitely much harder to place. It was too bad. Many people wanted a big dog, but by the time the puppy grew up, the owners realized it was no longer so much fun and a whole lot of work and expense. That was the kill age for so many animals. They got dumped at shelters, kicked out of the house and even left somewhere along the highway. It was sad the things animals went through with their owners. Some humans just didn't deserve to have pets.

The minutes grew longer. She kept distracting herself with more thoughts about animals and coming up with ideas where she could potentially find a home for both males. The longer it took Flynn to return, the harder it was for her to not think about him and what he was possibly doing.

When a tree branch cracked close by, she froze. Instantly, the two larger dogs bounded to their feet and barked. The smaller ones came closer to her. She glanced around, but really had no other place to go. She could race to the side of the shed and just keep going around in circles, but that would hardly be the answer.

And suddenly Flynn was there. "Sorry if I scared you," he said.

She bounded to her feet and cried, "Of course you did. You took off and didn't tell me anything, and then you didn't come back for so long only to break a branch before stepping out from behind a tree to terrify us all."

He stared at her, then pushed her back against the shed and covered her with his body. "Where was the crack?"

She pointed wordlessly to the back corner of the building.

He creeped to the far side and peered around the edge. Then he disappeared again.

She was getting fed up with him doing that.

When he came around the same way he'd approached the first time, she sighed with relief.

"Nothing's there," he said.

"And the sniper?"

"No sign of him."

"Of course not." She ran her hand through her hair, staring down at the animals. "I'm not sure I want to leave them out here anymore."

"Do you want to bring them into the house?"

"Will they be any safer?" She looked at him, then back down at the four dogs. It was a precedent she'd been avoiding. "I want to go inside and call someone I had in mind for the two little ones."

"Then let's get them inside."

With him leading the two larger dogs on leashes, she picked up the smaller ones, and they quickly made their way into the back of the house. She stepped inside, set down the dogs and motioned for him to close the door so they wouldn't run out. The dogs set about exploring the place.

She turned, looking around. "It just doesn't feel like home anymore."

"Anytime, when somebody breaks in," he said, "it's a violation that hits the very heart of you."

"LEVI SUGGESTED YOU head out with me. He wants me in another part of Texas to follow up on some inquiries to be made. He suggested it would be a good chance for you to get out of here."

She turned to look at him. "But I can't leave the animals alone."

"Logan said he'd stay."

"And how will that help?"

"It's just one of the many options we were considering. Another was for me to leave but in fact, sneak back inside to help look after the place, which would give the killer a chance to come in, thinking you were alone. But any effort we make to draw him out isn't a guaranteed success."

"Sounds like a guaranteed failure to me. I'm the one who's likely to get hurt."

He shook his head. "I won't allow that."

She sighed. "But this guy came here before and killed Jonas."

"And that brings up another issue. Any idea why Jonas was here?"

She flopped down into the kitchen chair. "I have no idea. Wish I could figure that out. For all I know Jonas was working with this guy."

Flynn had been on his way to the window. He turned and stared at her. "Is that likely? Did he have friends?"

"I think he had a few. But he always talked about this one guy and how the two of them would score big. Then Jonas could donate his share of the money to help out with the animals."

"Whoa. Tell me more. Wait ..." He pulled out his phone and called Levi. "Hang on, Anna has something to say." He turned on the speaker, laid the phone on the table and said, "Go ahead, Anna."

"I was just telling Flynn that Jonas said he'd met up with a guy, together they would make a big score, and when Jonas got lots of money, he would help out around my place. I just wondered if Jonas and the killer had been working together."

"Did he give you a description or any way to identify this man?" Levi asked.

"No, not really. Just that he'd met him at the center."

"What center?"

"It's a kind of a community center where people help unemployed individuals get jobs or for retirees to fill their spare time with volunteer work. It's one of those humanitarian places where you can do something to improve yourself."

"Name?"

"I'm not sure exactly. Back on Your Feet or something like that." Her voice trailed off. She shrugged at Flynn. "I'm sorry. I just don't remember."

"Don't worry," Levi said. "We'll find it. We know that Brendan was doing volunteer work. His brother was particularly happy about that."

There was a pause on the phone, as if Levi was writing down notes. They could hear scratching on paper. "I'll give him a quick call. He might even know the name of the center. Good work, Anna. If you remember anything else, let us know." And he hung up.

She glanced at Flynn. "Is he always like that? So abrupt?"

"When it's business, yes. Do you think Jonas's mother would know what the place is called?"

"No, I don't think so. He told me he had a separate entrance downstairs, and his mom lived upstairs. As if somehow that made it different than living in his mom's house."

Flynn grabbed his phone and sent a text. "I'll just let Levi know. I doubt we'll be allowed into Jonas's living quarters, but the police should have gone through it already."

"We can go ask his mom," she said slowly. "I can make up some kind of an excuse. I don't know, maybe he had some pictures or something of mine."

He studied her intently for a long moment and then nodded. "That's not a bad idea." He sent off another text to Levi with an update. Then turned to her and asked, "What about the dogs? Do we leave them in or out?"

"I'd rather leave them in."

"Good call. Grab your jacket. Let's go. We'll stop at Jonas's place to see if we can get in and take a look around. Then we'll head to the grocery store or for a meal first. I've been starving for hours now."

Chapter 9

A T JONAS'S MOTHER'S house, Anna walked, keys in hand to the downstairs living quarters, nodding at Flynn. "Her name is Evelyn," Anna announced. "She doesn't mind us taking a look. She's having a hard time with what happened. She appreciates anybody coming by." Anna was really sad for that. The meeting had been tough as it was. Evelyn had been almost pathetically grateful that someone cared enough to stop by. "She said Jonas had been very odd at the best of times, but the last few weeks he seemed a bit more over the top. She'd wondered if he was doing drugs."

"Did he have a history of it?"

Anna nodded. "He was a regular user, I believe. He offered to share at one point." She shrugged. "It was just part of who he was."

She unlocked the door to the downstairs suite and pushed it open. And froze. The place had been trashed. Everything was upside down and dumped. "Oh, boy."

Flynn stepped in behind her and closed the door. And again he pulled out his phone and called Levi. "We're at Jonas's place. It's been trashed. Don't know if someone was looking for something, but it'd be damn hard to find out what now."

Anna left him standing where he was and made her way into the kitchen. It wasn't as destroyed as the living room.

However, it was a mess with food all over the place. Wow. Did people really live like this? Did Evelyn know? This wouldn't be fun to clean out. Leftover take-out, coffee cups—both empty and not, from various coffeehouses—littered the table. Enough pizza boxes were on the table to feed several men. For a few days.

Carrying on, she pushed open the door to the master bedroom with her boot. Inside was messy, but not like the living room. The clothing was disheveled on the open shelving, but at least it wasn't on the floor. Then her focus landed on the bed. Instantly, she called out, "Flynn, come here."

When she didn't hear his steps, she walked back into the living room to Flynn, standing in the middle of the room, still talking on the phone, and she motioned for him to follow.

"Levi, I'll call you back." He ended the call and asked, "What's up?"

She pointed to the bedroom.

He stepped in, glanced around, his eyes landing on the bed. "Oh."

"Someone has been staying here with Jonas from the looks of it. What's the chance it's the killer?"

"Given this mess, I would have said no. But now that I see that bed ... made up military style and damn clean in comparison ..." He turned to look at her. "Did Jonas have any military training?"

She shook her head. "No idea."

"This does not match up with the rest of his living space." He turned to look at the kitchen.

She pointed at the coffee cups. "Beside the fact that whoever was here wasn't a housekeeper, the cups came in

86

twos. Not just one set either, but three sets on the table."

"So Jonas and someone."

"Unless Jonas was already dead, and we're looking for two others. But this could be the man that Jonas was talking about."

"Let's hope the police have swabbed this place for fingerprints." But he looked around and saw no evidence a crime scene forensic team had been here. And that made no sense to him. He quickly sent a text to Levi explaining what they had. He took several photos and forwarded them. "We need to find out why not."

"I can ask his mom." She walked back to the front door and headed upstairs. She knocked on the door again to see Jonas's mother. "Here are the keys. I promise to lock up when we leave. But I wonder, have the police not been here yet?"

"Yes," she said. "They have been. They came and got fingerprints from his bedroom and everything up here."

"What? I thought Jonas lived downstairs."

"Jonas *was*," his mom corrected. "But not for the last few weeks. He had a friend down there off and on, one who liked to be alone as much as possible, so Jonas started to sleep upstairs much of the time. I haven't seen or heard anybody down there for days." Tears came to her eyes again. "Everything is just so confusing now. I don't know who it was. But once I told the police another man was living downstairs, they didn't seem too interested. They wrote down the info but wanted to see Jonas's bedroom up here."

"Would you mind if I took a look too?" Anna pulled out her phone and quickly sent Flynn a text, telling him to get upstairs and join her.

At Jonas's bedroom door, his mom said, "You're welcome to look around, just don't take anything."

"Of course not," Anna said with a smile. "I'm sure you want to keep his things."

His mom shook her head. "I have no idea what I'm gonna do."

Anna wasn't sure she should warn Evelyn about the state of the rooms downstairs. As long as it was all part of the crime scene, she didn't think she could do anything yet. Then again the police didn't seem to feel the downstairs apartment was of interest to anyone. She opened the door to Jonas's bedroom and stepped inside.

And it was like a time warp. Posters from *Back to the Future* were on the wall. What looked like high school awards and mementos were all over the shelves.

At the sound of voices she turned to see Flynn talking with Jonas's mom outside the doorway. He stepped inside with a smile for Anna. "Did you find anything?"

Checking that Jonas's mom was down the hallway, Anna said, "It's still like a kid's room."

Flynn stopped and took a good look around and nodded. "Stunted growth?"

"He was immature in many ways. But how much of it was because he was always on drugs?" She opened her arms to the room. "But this kind of explains it a bit. Maybe he did have a mental illness and never quite matured past a specific point."

"Or this is his world before drugs. And the apartment downstairs is his world after." He nodded at the desk that was perfectly clean. "Just think about the apartment downstairs. Often drugs don't affect people in this way, but when it becomes the dominant factor in somebody's life, to the point they're addicted and no longer functioning well in society, often their surroundings no longer matter. What does is getting that next fix."

"He might have been getting to that stage, but I don't know for sure," she murmured in a low voice. The last thing she wanted was for Jonas's mother to hear them. This had to be hard enough without realizing to what extent your son had fallen.

She walked to his night table and pulled open the drawer. She didn't have hope of finding anything important, not once the police had been here. The drawer was empty. The shelf below it was too. She bent down on her hands and knees and checked under the bed. Outside of dust bunnies, it was also clean. She didn't really know what she was looking for, just something that would help her identify who the new person was that had been living downstairs. But then, why would that information be up here? Still she forced herself to go through the motions and checked everything she could.

In the closet she saw one of the coats Jonas wore on a regular basis. She pulled it out and turned to Flynn. "He wore this almost every time I saw him. Odd he wasn't when he was shot."

"So maybe he was living in this room toward the end, if his favorite clothes are here."

She shrugged. "Or he left it upstairs, and his mother hung it up for him."

She returned it where she'd found it, then checked the pockets. She pulled out a crumpled piece of paper—a receipt for fast food from three days before. She handed it to Flynn and went systematically back to the coat again. In the inside pocket she pulled out a small slip of paper, with a phone number and name, one she recognized. She spun and held it up for Flynn. "Is this the guy you were talking about?"

FLYNN STARED AT the note in Anna's hand. Confirmation. Something he hadn't really expected to see. He reached out and took it, looking at both sides. It was torn from a store advertisement, a local one here in town.

He pulled out his phone and dialed the handwritten number on the reverse side. The phone rang multiple times. Not waiting to see if anything else happened, he hung up, then dialed Levi. He quickly updated him, adding, "Can somebody put a trace on this number and see what we get?"

"We're on it," Levi said. "We'll also check the police files for that address."

"Good idea. If there's been any disturbances at that address, the neighbors would probably know something." He stared out the window and said, "I think after I'm done in this room, maybe we'll talk to a couple neighbors here and see what they might have to say."

"Good idea. Touch base in, say, thirty minutes." Levi ended the call.

With a last glance around, he motioned toward the doorway. "Are you ready to go?"

She nodded. "Nothing else of interest appears to be here."

They walked back out, thanking Jonas's mom for letting them see his room.

Back outside, Anna asked, "What was that about going door-to-door?"

"We should check with the neighbors and see if they saw Brendan. Somebody should've seen something."

"Wouldn't the police have asked?"

"Would they? As far as they were concerned, a friend was staying downstairs in the apartment. They didn't seem to care about the other guy. Then again, it's not like the police have much time to worry about this case."

"But we do." Resolutely, she walked across to the first house beside Jonas's mother's place. She knocked on the door. When an older woman came out, Anna quickly explained that she was a friend of Jonas's and wondered if the woman had seen anything suspicious in the last few days.

The neighbor shook her head. "Jonas has always been a bit suspicious on his own. But since he started hanging out with that creep..." She shook her head. "He's just been on a downhill slide. I'm not surprised he was murdered."

Inwardly agreeing with the woman but needing to keep her talking, Anna said, "Have you seen other people around here lately?"

"A black truck. Don't know the man. But it was parked in the front a lot."

"Any chance you know the license plate?" Flynn asked from behind Anna. "Even just a letter or two?"

The lady shook her head. "It always came in the dark and was gone in the morning. It gave me the creeps actually. It's kind of ghostlike."

She gave Flynn a hard glance.

"Nothing good ever comes of people who only come and leave in the dark. Definitely shenanigans going on in that place," he said.

"Well, hopefully that's all over with now," Anna said gently. "The neighborhood should be safe again."

"*Harrumph*. I hope so." And the woman closed the door in their face.

Flynn proceeded to check with the other neighbors, but everybody said the same thing. Large black truck, nobody had seen the license plate. As for the driver, no one saw him.

The only extra information they got was the truck was full-size, solid black, with no contrasting trim, obvious bed liner, or canopy. As far as being helpful, it wasn't much. This was Texas—everyone had trucks.

When they were done and walking back to Anna's car, Levi called. "The phone is registered to Brendan McAllister. And it's a Houston number."

With his breath coming out in a gush, Flynn said, "That's the best confirmation we've had yet."

"This is good stuff," Levi said. "That puts Brendan together with Jonas. We can already place Jonas at the house. If we can place Brendan there too, that would lock it down."

"Do we have motive? Means wouldn't be too hard, as Brendan is a weapons specialist."

"Right. I should phone the cops and see if we can confirm the murder weapon. He's unlikely to be so stupid as to use his own gun, but..." Levi's tone changed. "What are you two doing now?"

Flynn turned to look at Anna. "We need to stop at a grocery store, and then we'll be back at the house."

"Staying there for the night? The others are planning to leave soon. Except Logan, he's staying at his father's for the evening. This would be your last call for a ride home until then."

"Good to know. Thanks. I'll touch base with Logan later." He ended the call and turned to face Anna. "Groceries?"

She nodded. "I'm starved."

Chapter 10

S HE WALKED UP the steps, unlocked the door, picked up the two bags she'd brought from the car and headed to the kitchen. The dogs barked and milled around her in joy. She put the groceries on the table, then reached out to give them each a big hug. "So how was it being inside, guys?"

She glanced around, but it appeared they hadn't had any accidents. For that she was grateful. At least they had each other for company. She could put them back in their cages, but that didn't appeal.

"I'll cook tonight if you want to put stuff away," Anna said.

Flynn nodded and gave her a smile.

She checked the answering machine to find that her earlier phone call had resulted in something very positive. The couple would come by this evening to look at the two little dogs, if that was okay with her. She picked up the phone and called them back. "I'll be here this evening if you can give me a time."

The man said, "How about right after dinner. Maybe six thirty?"

"Perfect." She put away the phone in a much happier frame of mind, then began a chicken Caesar salad for each of them. She snagged the garlic bread, prepped it, set it aside to go in at the end. It would give them some substance to go with the salad.

Flynn was a big man. He had already demonstrated a decent appetite. She didn't have anywhere near the appetite he did, but she was starved. Right now, she could eat both his meal and hers. As soon as she got the chicken breasts in the oven, she called out, "The couple is coming tonight to take a look at the two little dogs."

"That's great," Flynn said. "You should take a walk down there to ensure the cats are okay."

She shot him a horrified look and raced outside.

"Sorry! Didn't mean to make you panic."

"The last thing I need is something else happening around here," she said.

Flynn followed her. "Hey, since Jonas's body was found here, and with the police presence off and on, we probably don't have to worry about Brendan showing tonight. No guarantees, but just saying…" When she nodded at him, he sauntered back to the kitchen.

She arrived at the cages and opened the cat door to find everybody still where they belonged. The four dogs had followed behind her, and the smaller ones barking like crazy. Jimbo stuffed his nose against the glass of the cat door. She reached down and hooked a leash on each of the two little ones and took them out on the small dog run. With any luck they would have a new home tonight. She walked the other two out to the back dog run and set them free. They needed an hour or so to themselves.

None of the animals appeared to be disturbed or upset. She'd take that as a good sign there was no intruder around. The cats would need food soon. As she headed toward them, Flynn was already outside again, saying, "Don't worry about it. I'll feed the cats now. You worry about dinner."

That worked for her.

When Flynn was done, he walked inside, sniffed the air experimentally and said, "That smells good."

She smiled at him. "Just like old times."

"It sure is."

When he'd been here before, they'd taken turns cooking meals. She did a tastier pasta, but he cooked a better steak.

She sat down, checking her watch. "We have twenty minutes to eat before the couple arrives."

"It's all good."

She settled in to enjoy her chicken Caesar salad. She glanced at Flynn to find him halfway through his meal. When she was done, she started the dishes. Before she got the sink filled, Flynn said, "Remember our *old times*? If you cooked, I cleaned, and we switched off as needed. Go deal with paperwork in case they want the dogs tonight."

At that reminder, she headed to her office to grab some adoption papers. There was nothing wrong with feeling positive. It had been a hell of a day already. If she could find homes for these two, it would be perfect.

An hour later, she realized it had been the best day she'd had in a long time. Tears were in her eyes as she watched the couple take the two little dogs out to their car and place them in the backseat.

Flynn walked out and put an arm around her shoulder, tugging her close. "Nice job."

She sniffed and wiped the tears from her eyes. "It's so good to see them leave, going to a good home, but it's also damn hard."

He laughed. "They are yours when they are here. But, like all babies, they have to grow up and move on."

"I really need to do something to help the cats now too.

We're down to just the two large dogs, a hamster, snake, rabbit, and four cats."

"You barely have enough animals to call yourself a shelter anymore. It's a good time to shut it down, if that's what you need to do."

"Now that I have the money, that's not gonna happen," she said robustly, once again buoyed by success. "What I need to do is contact the other shelters and see how many animals need to be rescued before they hit the kill door."

"And then you'll take them in, I suppose," Flynn said with a knowing smile.

"That's what I'm here for," she said. "Maybe with some of that money, I can afford to get an assistant. Someone to help."

"I'm sure you can," he said. "How many animals can you actually take here?"

"With the new pens that I have yet to use, I could probably take in close to forty dogs. The problem is finding homes for them. But they all go eventually. It's just a matter of time. People are always more easily suckered in if they see the animal at events. Those who call me are the ones who have been out looking. I do have a website obviously, and that takes a bit of work too. But now I get to update it, let them know that both little dogs have a new home." She reached up and kissed him briefly on the cheek. "I'll do that right now." And she bolted into the office.

LIKE AN IDIOT, Flynn stood in the hallway, a hand to his cheek. It was the first sign of affection she'd actually shown him since his return. And he was loving it. Obviously, today was one of the highlights of the week, if not the whole month, for her. A sizable check, two animals adopted and she was safe, so far. Plus, the police were done and gone, taking whatever mess they were dealing with. Now if only they could figure out where the hell Brendan was and put a stop to any shenanigans he was up to.

While she was in the office, he pulled out his phone. "Levi, any update?"

"No, I'm still tracking down Brendan's whereabouts. His brother swears he's been at his place for the last two days, but he has a small cottage in the back where Brendan's been staying. So he can't actually confirm that he's been there—in fact, he's hardly seen him for several weeks."

"I can pretty well damn confirm that he hasn't, but was at Jonas's place," Flynn said shortly. "It just feels like he's planning something, but I don't know what it is. I don't want him to target the animals here either."

"No, none of us do."

After ending the call, he walked to the kitchen and put on a pot of coffee. He couldn't shake the feeling that something was brewing in the atmosphere. If he looked at this as Brendan wanting payback, what he had done so far wasn't enough.

Just as the coffee finished dripping, he heard a knock on the front door. He opened it to two policemen standing on the porch. He nodded. "Good evening. What can we do to help you?"

The first officer introduced himself. "I'm Detective Baker. I believe you are Flynn Kilpatrick, correct?"

He nodded. "Yes."

"We need you to come down to the station to answer some questions."

His eyebrows shot up. "Is there any reason I can't answer

them here?"

The two men stepped slightly backward to allow him to step out onto the porch. Baker said, "We would like to see you at the station."

Flynn didn't like the sound of that at all.

"Let me grab my jacket and tell Anna." He didn't give them a chance to refuse.

He turned and walked into the kitchen, grabbed his jacket from the back of the chair and headed to the office.

Anna was working on the computer. She looked up with a big smile. "Hey, do I smell coffee?"

"Yeah, but you'll be drinking alone. The police are here, and they want me at the station for questioning."

Her gaze widened. "What?" She bounded to her feet and raced to the front door. "What do you want with Flynn?" she asked the detectives.

"We just have some questions to ask him."

"Then why the station? You could come in and ask what you need."

Both men shook their heads. "We are requesting his presence at the station."

She crossed her arms and jutted out her chin.

Flynn grabbed her by the shoulder. "Don't worry. I'll go with them. I don't have anything to hide."

"That might be," she said, "but you're not going alone. I'm coming too. I'll drive and follow you." She glared at the two cops. "Make sure you keep him safe. He's already been shot at once. And there better not be one damn bruise on him by the time I see him at the station."

Flynn laughed. "They can't beat me up, sweetie." He bent down and dropped a kiss on her temple. "But it's a good idea for you to follow me there. I don't want you alone here."

She raced into the kitchen and was back out with her keys, jacket, and purse. Turning to lock the front door, she headed to the car as he got into the backseat of the cruiser.

As he sat inside, he watched her follow them down the street. He smiled. He really didn't like this development; it made her worry about him. Well, something was good about that. At least it proved she cared. He quickly texted Levi and gave him an update.

Then he phoned Logan. "Interesting development."

Logan answered, "No worries. We'll send a lawyer over."

"Don't need one," Flynn said comfortably. "I didn't do anything."

"Yes, but somebody's out to get you, so the more support you have at the onset, the less chance you have of anybody pushing your buttons."

"I'm just not sure how much to tell them about Brendan."

"Another reason for the lawyer. We'll meet you there."

Flynn ended the call and stared at his phone. He might have had a crappy time this past year, but he never doubted his friends. It had taken a long time to get to this point with his position at Legendary Security and to where he was with Anna at present. He had no intention of blowing it now. No matter what Brendan might have planned, they'd have to go on without Flynn. Because he and Anna had a future, and it didn't include jail time.

Chapter 11

"YOU CAN TAKE a seat on the side, ma'am." The detective was polite.

She gave him a hard glance and said, "I'd rather sit with Flynn."

"He's just answering questions. You can wait until he comes back out again."

She crossed her arms over her chest and glared at the man on the other side of the desk. "I know you're just doing your job," she said.

"Good," he barked. "Then let us do it. If there's no reason to keep him, then we won't."

She glared at him again until a soft laugh came from behind her. She turned to see Logan. "There you are. You're getting him out of here, right?"

"With you on his defense team?" Logan asked with a chuckle. "I doubt they'll charge him with anything. Because if they did, they'd have to face you. And believe me, that's not what any of them want."

The detective behind the desk muttered, "You got that right."

Logan led her to one of the long benches against the wall. "Let's just sit here and relax."

"How can I possibly do that when they took him in for questioning?"

"Did they say what it was about?" he asked.

"No, but what else could it be other than Jonas's murder?" She let her breath out in a heavy sigh, running her hands through her hair. "The guy makes me nuts. You know that, right?"

Logan laughed. "He has that effect on a lot of people."

She smiled. "But he's a good guy."

"Glad you noticed."

It was the emphasis on the word *noticed* in his voice that had her glaring at him in suspicion. "What do you mean by that?"

His grin widened. "Flynn likes you too."

"Oh," she said in a small voice. "Was it that obvious?"

He laughed out loud. "Your defense of him says a lot."

"You've got to remember I defend the underdogs," she told him.

"That's true. But Flynn really doesn't need anybody to stand up for him."

"I'm afraid he does now. I don't know what the hell that friend of his is up to, but he won't be happy until Flynn suffers for some reason."

"Well, he's not a friend any longer," Logan said. "I'm not sure they ever really were. But they were in the same unit. And when things go bad, they tend to go really bad. Nobody in the military has a weak character, they don't breed them that way. When they find strengths, they hone and sharpen them. So when two military types get on opposite sides of the same bar, it can get ugly."

"He has to really hate Flynn in order to want him to suffer like this."

"I wouldn't be at all surprised if he isn't planning to kill him."

"Oh, my God," she cried. "Really?"

Logan grabbed her hands, already twisted into knots, her nails digging into her soft flesh. "I shouldn't have said that. Just take it easy. We really don't know anything yet."

"No, you're wrong there. We know somebody's setting him up. And with that much hate inside, there's really no way to know when they'll stop. If they're gonna stop. I think you're right. The endgame is to take Flynn out."

"Even if it is, Flynn is not anybody's easy endgame."

"And he's not alone, right?" She stared at Logan as if willing him to give her the answer she needed.

Logan nodded his head. "He has all of Levi's company, me, and my father. And that's considerable. If we have to, we can pull Bullard's team into this."

"Who's Bullard?"

Logan shook his head. "I forgot you don't know who he is. Another guy running a company like Levi's, but they're over in Africa."

"Sounds as if I'd like him if he'd step up and help Flynn out. I don't think Flynn's had so many people stand by him lately."

"No, he hasn't. He doesn't have any family. But I've been his best friend for as long as I can remember."

She nodded. "He's got a chip on his shoulder. That I-don't-need-anybody-in-my-life-because-I'm-doing-just-fine chip."

At that Logan laughed out loud. "I see you do know him, and obviously very well."

His tone held a bit of suggestiveness. She flushed. "Not that way."

"But soon," he teased.

She flushed an even brighter red and glared at him. "Not

likely. The last thing I need to do is spend my evenings sitting inside the police station, waiting for him to come out."

"Especially when you can be doing something so much more fun." And he chuckled again.

He obviously knew Flynn very well too. Maybe too well, from the looks he was giving her. "How long have you known him?" she asked abruptly.

"Decades," he said cheerfully. "We had a few years apart where we didn't have anything to do with each other but hooked up again in the military. That was awesome."

She shook her head. "So you know all about his history with women then."

"Of course I do. Doesn't mean I know the details or about all of them. But I know about you."

She nodded. "Figures."

"Why?"

"Because I have no intention of being yet another little notch on Flynn's bedpost."

"Now that is not something Flynn ever did. He had some short-term romances, but when he's with a girl, he's in 100 percent. That didn't mean it always worked out obviously, as he's never been married. But his relationships always lasted six months or longer."

She turned to look at him. "For real?"

He nodded. "SEALs get a bad reputation. Hell, all military men get a bad name for being more into the wild and crazy one-night stands and weekends," he said. "And I doubt any of us can say that we haven't done something that makes us look back and cringe. But Flynn was much more circumspect. He wasn't into one-night stands—he was into relationships. I give him credit. I thought he was gonna make it with a couple of them. But it's tough being married to a SEAL."

"It's tough being married to any military man," she said. "There is always danger around you. Not knowing if you'll ever come back from the latest mission."

"True enough. And you gotta realize Flynn's doing the same kind of work. Maybe not quite as dangerous. Hell, maybe it's more so. I'm fairly new with Levi myself. But it's the kind of work we used to do. And some of it's hazardous."

"Aren't you the one who looks after the rich and famous?"

Logan gave her a flat stare. "No. I might've done a job or two like that, but that's definitely not where my aptitude lies."

"You sure? You look like the one who prefers to have some of those gorgeous women throw themselves all over you."

Logan chuckled. "Those gorgeous women throw themselves all over me whether I'm looking after them or not."

"Maybe you lost your heart to one of those fancy ladies you were guarding."

She couldn't help teasing him, but she knew that chances were none of it was even true. Until she saw a flush rise up his neck. It was her turn to give him a flat stare and say, "Come on, Logan. Give me the details. Who was she?"

He glared at her. "No one."

She snickered. "Wait until I tell Flynn about this."

He narrowed his gaze, shoved his face a little closer to hers and said in a mock-threatening voice, "You won't say a word to him."

She shoved her face right back into his until her nose was almost touching his. "Yeah, you wanna bet?"

FLYNN WATCHED THE two spit at each other. He couldn't stop grinning. His friends were great. He stood in front of them for a long moment, waiting for them to notice him. When they didn't, he cleared his throat.

Both turned to look up at Flynn, his arms crossed over his chest, a big smirk on his face. "How nice you two are getting to know each other."

"I'm sure she has a crush on you," Logan said with a big smirk. "I told her that she should find somebody else because you're a busy man with the ladies these days."

Flynn's eyebrows shot up.

"That's okay. You don't understand why he's being mean and lying. Logan is missing his sweetheart," Anna said, her voice supersweet. "That's what happens when you're dumped by someone prettier than you." She turned to glare at Logan.

Flynn broke into raucous laughter. "Oh, my God. Seeing you two like this is perfect." He grabbed an arm on each of them, pulled them to their feet and said, "Shall we leave now?"

Anna turned and stopped. "Can you leave? Oh, that's wonderful." She threw her arms around him and gave him a big hug. "I was so worried about you."

"I told you there was no need. It's all fine."

She stepped back a bit and glared at him. "In my world, there's no *all fine*. But I sure as hell would like to get out of here." She turned to look at Logan, saying in a half-grudging voice, "You're welcome to come back to my place for a drink—coffee or something—if you want."

Logan's grin flashed. "Only as long as you don't bring up any more of our girlfriend or boyfriend issues."

She thrust her chin forward. "As long as you don't either."

Flynn snagged each of them by the arm once again and directed them toward the front door. "Damn it, that must've been some conversation while you were waiting for me." They walked outside. "I'm sorry I missed it."

"I could've missed it easily." Anna rolled her eyes. But she was just so damn happy Flynn was allowed to go and there appeared to be no repercussions from the police visit. "What did they actually want?"

They were headed across the parking lot where their vehicles waited. She walked to her car and waited for him to answer.

"Someone sent them a letter stating I killed Jonas."

Her jaw dropped.

Logan exploded with, "Are you serious?"

Flynn nodded. "But apparently the autopsy confirmed Jonas was killed while I was flying home. He was shot by a small caliber handgun. The slices on his arm were inflicted with my knife and more for show than anything else. More forensic evidence to nail my coffin closed. But I wasn't here so the plan didn't work. The same thing for the rifle. Jonas was shot with it postmortem. But it wasn't the murder weapon. They are looking for a handgun for that. And of course, they found a partial print of mine on the rifle." He glanced at Logan and said, "Thank God I went on that trip with you and Harrison."

"Jesus." Logan stared off in the distance, then shook his head. "Somebody has it in for you."

"Not somebody, it's Brendan. I'm pretty damn sure."

"So sure you'll exclude everybody else in that equation?" Anna asked. "Making assumptions is not the best idea."

"No, it's not, but nobody else in my world really hates me like that. And I told the police that this time."

"I think one of the things about it is that we don't often recognize who it is that hates us. The world is full of lies and liars."

"True enough. But most of those liars aren't willing to go through with murder to make a point."

"Aren't the police looking for Brendan? Why aren't they asking him where he was on the weekend Jonas was killed?"

"They are looking for him. And as soon as they track him down, they will ask him just that," Flynn said. "But it appears Brendan is hiding out, and nobody knows where he is right now, including his brother."

"That sucks. We need to find him ourselves."

"That's what I was thinking," Flynn said. "We need to track his credit cards. He has to be paying his way somehow. However, if he was living at his brother's house or Jonas's, that's a different story. So when was his ATM last hit for cash? Does he have a credit card? When was it last used?"

"I believe Ice is getting those answers."

"When we go home, I'll see if I can get more." He glanced at the two of them and asked, "Are you coming to Anna's place?"

Logan nodded. "I'll follow you."

Anna unlocked and opened the car, standing on the pavement, waiting. She turned back to Flynn and asked, "You want to drive, or are you okay if I do?"

"I wouldn't mind driving," he said amiably. "But if it's an issue for you, go ahead."

"I'm tired," she admitted. "If you want to, that would be fine with me." She walked around the car, handed the keys to him and got into the passenger side of her small car.

He walked around, got into the driver's side and turned on the engine. When they were both buckled in, he drove the car out onto the road. Behind them, Logan followed in one of the big company trucks.

"How many trucks does Levi actually have at the compound?"

"Half a dozen by now, I think. Also a Suburban or two and a couple cars."

"I gather business is good."

Flynn laughed. "It is, but one never really knows how good."

"Can't blame him for that," Anna said. "He probably doesn't even know. With so many jobs coming and going, you're really only gonna have facts and figures after a few months. As long as the cash is flowing inward, and you're covering everything, then you're doing fine. To know if there's anything left at the end of the day, well, that'll take a couple quarters to get an idea."

"What was that about Logan having a ladylove who dumped him?"

She shrugged. "He was razzing me about how you and I interact, so I returned it about him being dumped. Got quite a rise out of him too. I think something must have happened between him and a woman he was looking after in California."

"I'll have to ask about that," Flynn said. "Logan doesn't get involved easily."

"Yeah, I got that impression. He said the same thing about you. And that when you do, it's generally for a long-term relationship."

"I try hard. If one is worth starting, I'll give it my all and see how we do." He glanced at her. "How about you? You go into relationships in a lighthearted manner?"

"No." She stared out into the darkness on the other side of the windshield. "But then, I haven't had the number of relationships you have."

"It doesn't matter how many we have." His voice deepened. "When you're in a relationship, you give it your all. There are no guarantees in life, or the future. There certainly aren't any in happiness. All we can do is our best."

She turned to look at him and smiled. "How very true."

He made a couple right-hand turns, then headed out onto the highway. This was one way to get back to her place, probably the fastest. The turnoff was just a mile down the road. Just as they approached it, he put on the signal and slowed down.

Anna glanced behind to see if Logan was there. A big truck was following them, but it wasn't Logan's. "Uhm ..."

"I see it." Flynn's voice turned grim and hard. "Hold on."

The truck came whipping right up against the back bumper of her car. Flynn hit the gas, and instead of taking the right turn to get off the highway, he darted between two cars in the second lane, and they moved over to the turning lane on the far side as well. She twisted to look at the truck. It was cutting across too. "Oh, my God, it's following us."

"I think he was running us off the road."

Flynn took a hard corner too fast in front of oncoming traffic, then jumped through the lanes to take the turn on the far side. She gave a small cry.

"Sorry, but I had to get out of there." He whipped onto the first right and took a series of turns, shaking off the tail. Finally, he pulled into a small residential block and parked. The two of them sat there, staring at each other for a long moment. Then both at the same time turned to look behind them. There was no sign of the truck.

"Did I just imagine that?"

He shook his head. "I sure as hell didn't."

"What about Logan?"

Flynn pulled out his phone and called Logan. There was no answer. "Damn it. Best case scenario, Logan followed the truck and is right now tracking it down. Worst, Logan missed the whole thing."

No, that would be that the truck took out Logan first. But he hadn't heard or seen anything happening behind him, so he presumed Logan's luck was still holding. That guy seemed to walk through a fire and come out smiling and smelling fresh as roses on the other side. Flynn had never known anybody else like Logan.

Into the eerie silence she whispered, "What do we do?"

Chapter 12

S HE HAD THE answer to that question a few minutes later. Somehow, from a completely different direction, they arrived at the shelter. Everything looked the same from outside. She had literally grabbed her purse as she'd bolted after Flynn and the police. Now she stared at the house, wondering if the asshole who'd followed them had been here first.

She had to check on her animals. She hopped out of the car and approached the front door. Everything looked the same as she'd left it. She unlocked the door and walked inside with Flynn right at her heels.

She knew he was still phoning Logan. The fact that there was no answer really bothered him. Her too. She'd hate for somebody else to get hurt. She didn't care who this guy was after, he had no business taking out anyone.

She'd left the dogs in the dog run. The house appeared to be fine. Keeping close to Flynn, they walked out to check the animals.

The cats were sleeping, not even noticing she'd been gone, she suspected. The dogs barked as soon as they heard them approach. Once they saw it was Flynn and Anna, they barked in joy, jumping and whining. She opened the pen and walked inside, bending down to give both a cuddle, still missing the little ones she'd found a good home for earlier.

She still had her evening work to do. The rabbit and hamster needed pellets and new hay for their cages. And the snake— maybe Flynn would feed him.

"Let's get this dealt with," she said quietly. "Hopefully by that time, Logan will show up."

"I'm calling Levi first." He walked a few steps away and connected with somebody from the compound.

She turned her attention back to the animals. She had so few here right now. She quickly changed the hamster's sawdust, gave it fresh water and food, did the same for the rabbit and walked into the cat house.

She sat down on the floor, and the cats came over for attention. As much she liked to believe they were fine on their own, they needed human contact just as much as any other animal. She wondered if she were up to having them all in the house. There were four here though. She could consider keeping them, the two dogs, hamster, and rabbit and be done with the shelter. No way would she keep the snake.

Her attitude to the place had changed. Since finding Jonas in the shed, it just wasn't the same anymore. Maybe what she needed was a different location, though that cost money. Not something she had a whole lot of. Her property was worth a lot more now than when she'd first bought it, and the area had grown up around her. It was also a large lot, and the developers would be all over her for it. If she moved out of town though, would it impact how many animals were adopted? She had no idea. It would certainly be a longer trip to the vet, but she didn't have to move that far.

That's when she first realized she was actually thinking of a place between here and the compound. The small towns around it were a lot cheaper. She could sell this parcel and buy something larger and better suited. Plus, set money aside. A lot could be said for being more financially stable. Of course all the cages would have to be rebuilt at the other end. Although a lot of them could be moved too. She could also add a few new pens, bigger and easily accessible.

For the first time she stood back and studied what she'd built here—the pens and dog runs. Replacing the building was one of the biggest concerns, because it had all the cages built inside, plus, she had an examination room in the back and several others for animals recovering from surgeries. To set up something like this all over again would be brutal.

She didn't know if she could do it.

On the other hand, if it was just the property keeping her here, that wasn't a good enough reason. There were better locations elsewhere. She had no place for visitors to come and see the animals; there was no parking out front, which was always an issue. The dogs could use a larger run. If she actually had a property upgrade, she could take in other animals when asked. She was one of the few with a lot of this size. But it certainly wasn't big enough for anything like goats or horses.

She shook her head. This was kind of a crossroad. And all because of Jonas.

Poor Jonas.

On that note she put the dogs on leashes. Flynn was still talking on the phone. She said in a low voice, "I'm taking the dogs for a walk."

She let herself out into the back alley and let the dogs roam. They loved this time of night. She didn't usually take them for too long a walk, not like the exercise they needed being the size they were. But the alleyway ran the full length of several properties on either side. All kinds of interesting smells were here for the dogs to follow.

She walked to the far end, giving them a chance to lift their legs and sniff around, with as much freedom as a dog could have on a leash.

As she walked back toward her property, Jimbo walked along the ditch in the alley on the far side. His head down, that little bit of hound in him had picked up the scent of something. Probably a rabbit or an owl, although Anna wouldn't be surprised at anything. She lived on the edge of the city, and though the properties were big, their owners weren't wealthy. Lots of people dumped their garbage in this alley. She never understood it. There was trash pickup every week. Why throw your shit in the back alley where it would never get collected?

As they approached the back gate, Jimbo refused to budge. She walked over to see what he'd found. If it was a skunk, she really didn't want him to come close to it. A flashlight in its eyes wasn't enough to get it moving. Oddly enough there was something on the ground. It looked like an old rag. She kicked it with her foot, and it flipped and moved over several inches to the side. Something gleamed in the night, but she couldn't see what it was.

She turned to look at Flynn. He stood at the gate, still talking on his phone. She gave a sharp whistle, which caused him to spin and look at her. She pointed at the ground. "Can you bring a light? I need to see what this is."

He unhitched some kind of a tool from his belt, clicked a button and there was a beam of light. He walked closer to her, stooped down on the side of the ditch in front of her. And swore.

"Shit," she said.

On the ground, mostly buried in the dirt and mud, was

a gun. And she had no doubt in her mind it was the gun that had been used to shoot Jonas.

FLYNN STARED DOWN at the handgun and said into the phone, "Levi, one of the dogs just found a gun in the alley behind Anna's place."

"Call the cops. Chances are it's planted evidence, but we have to follow this through the legal way."

"Yeah, that's what I figured."

He ended the call, looked at her and said, "I'll be calling the cops next."

She rolled her eyes and said, "Great. Like I haven't had enough of them yet." Anna took Jimbo and Duggy back into the dog pen.

He watched as she walked through the gate. Then he bent down to study the handgun. He didn't recognize it, thankfully. Although he could have potentially touched this one—several years ago—if it was Brendan's.

On their days off while in the military, they'd often go shooting. As he stared down at the small handgun, he realized it sat in a shitty spot with gasoline, mud, and dirt all around it, so who knew if any fingerprints were left to be found. But if this was Brendan's, then it could be one Flynn had held. Still, the cops knew he hadn't been in the country at the time of the killing.

He quickly called the cops and explained what he'd found.

"We'll send somebody out there within the hour," the dispatcher said. "Please stay with the object."

Right. Like he had nothing else to do. For his own sake, he took several photos and sent them to Levi for backup, and leaned against the fence on the far side. He stared at Anna's house for a long time. And then realized this position gave him a great insight into her life. Because he could see her as she left the kitchen, walked to the office, then into the other room where the dining table was, which meant anyone else could have stood exactly where he was and watched her— and him. He glanced down at his flashlight and checked the surrounding area.

Besides his own footprints, he could tell somebody had stood on the far side. The imprints were deep in the mud. They were also much bigger than his. And there were several cigarette butts around the immediate area.

Brendan wouldn't have been that sloppy. Not unless he thought it was a slam dunk that Flynn would get arrested for this murder.

Still, Flynn would point it out to the cops. And therefore, since he didn't want to trample through it, he waited.

Anna came out the back door. "You coming in?"

He shook his head. "The cops are on the way. I'll wait for them."

She frowned, then nodded. She returned a few minutes later with a hot cup of coffee.

He smiled at her. "Thank you for thinking of me."

As she walked away, she muttered, "I wish I could stop."

"I'd really rather you didn't."

She froze and spun around to see him. "Seriously?"

He nodded his head. "It's why I asked how you felt about relationships," he said, his voice low, deep. "Because I definitely want to take this further and see where we can go with it."

She took several steps toward him and whispered, "So do I. But I just didn't know if you were serious."

He reached out his free hand and gently brushed the stray strands of hair off her face. He tugged her a little bit closer and whispered, "When it comes to *you*, I'm always serious."

With the coffee cup in one hand, he wrapped his other arm around her. He dropped a kiss on her nose and forehead, then unable to help himself, he tilted her chin and gave her a slow, mind-drugging kiss to let her know just how serious he really was. When he lifted his head, she let out a happy sigh and snuggled up against his chest.

He held her close. "We'll get through this," he whispered. "Don't ever worry about that."

"I'm worried about a lot of things right now. And the fact that somebody wants you in jail for life is just one of them. What if he actually comes back and tries to hurt you?" She leaned back to look up at his face in the darkness. "Or worse, kill you."

"I'm not that easy to kill," he whispered, touched that she was so concerned.

"Nobody is invincible, nor can they argue with bullets all the time and get away with it."

She was so serious and sad. He just wanted to wrap her up and carry her upstairs and into bed, show her how good life could be. She'd been through a lot these last few weeks. Months. But there'd been good things too, and she needed to keep that in the forefront of her mind.

"True enough. And I know the danger right now. But my concern is keeping you safe."

She chuckled. "So I'll look after you, and you'll do the same for me."

He barked a laugh. "Sounds good to me."

With her holding him close, the two of them stood in

the alleyway for several long moments. Just as she was about to pull away, a vehicle arrived, headlights shining toward them.

She stiffened. "Are we assuming that's the cops?"

"I'm not sure yet. However, we are expecting them."

They pressed back against the fence. Some shrubbery stood between the two of them and the vehicle, but not enough to hide them if those lights were to shine in their direction.

As they waited for the vehicle to approach, another turned into the other end of the alleyway. This one was a bigger and higher, like a truck.

Anna gasped. "You think that's the one?"

"No idea." Now crouching down very low, pulling her down beside him, he said, "Get to your yard and inside the fence."

She did as he instructed. The truck appeared to be idling at the entrance to the alleyway. And that made it suspicious as hell. The car, on the other hand, was almost where Flynn waited.

But since he didn't know yet who the hell the killer was, he couldn't guarantee the car was anybody they wanted to see either. When it drove closer, he saw it was a cop car. The engine shut off; as were the lights, and two men got out. One was holding a big flashlight.

He shone the light on Flynn. "There you are. I was wondering what the hell you're hiding from."

Flynn motioned to the truck still sitting at the far end. "A truck almost ran us off the road earlier tonight on our way home from the police station. I managed to shake it, but now I'm wondering if that's it again."

The cops turned and studied the truck. The first quietly

said, "I'll go through the backyard and see if I can come up behind it."

He'd already slipped up against the fence. The second got into the driver seat of the car and backed it away. Around the front of the house, he turned as if to take the main part of the road, but instead he pulled a U-turn and went the other way. In the meantime, the first one rounded back to Flynn.

Flynn figured the truck would back out, make a run and disappear before the police car got there.

There was no way to tell how far the cop car would go. Flynn watched its headlights shining in the dark. Then it disappeared. Suddenly, it was up behind the truck which quickly hit the gas and raced forward; the cop was behind it.

The truck blasted past where Flynn and the other cop stood. No way to stop it. However, it slowed as it approached. The driver turned and stared directly at Flynn. And he knew him. It was Brendan. "Shit." He glared as Brendan disappeared in front of him.

"Did you recognize the truck?"

"Yes, it's the same one that tried to run us off the road earlier. And I recognized the driver. Brendan McAllister. He's the man I told the detectives about."

"Good. You let us handle this. We'll get this asshole off the road. And we have more than a few questions to ask, so don't leave."

He didn't know how they would handle it, but the cop car was right on Brendan's ass, sirens going. No way in hell would Brendan slow down or stop. "Even if you have a roadblock somewhere up ahead, this guy will crash through anything in his path."

"Yeah, I hear you." The cop turned back. "We came

here to pick up a gun. Where is it?"

Using the flashlight, Flynn pointed to it on the ground. It looked like it was even more covered in mud now. The cop reached down and with what looked like a pencil, collected it and put it in an evidence bag. He held it up in the concentrated light and said, "This could be the murder weapon."

"That's why I called you."

"Any chance it has your fingerprints on it?" The cop studied Flynn's face intently.

Because of that, Flynn kept his expression easy, natural. "If it's Brendan's, anything is possible. We were in the military together. We often would target practice in the woods. Not only did we need to keep that up for our jobs but it was fun. A great way to pass the time with the guys."

The cop stared from the gun to Flynn.

Flynn felt he had to add, "It's not mine."

"Good enough. You weren't driving the truck just now, so I'll take that as a sign of faith that you're not the guy who did this." He put the evidence in his jacket pocket as another car turned into the alleyway. "Here's my ride. We'll be in touch."

The second cop car pulled up beside them. The cop got into the vehicle, and they drove off. Flynn watched as they disappeared into the night. Good luck catching Brendan. That wouldn't be so easy. In his heart, he knew this guy would get away.

Chapter 13

FLYNN HAD SENT her inside when the police arrived. "Anna?"

"I'm in the office," she called out.

He stopped at the doorway. "What are you doing?"

"Going through the videos for the hours we were gone tonight," she said. "I just want to make sure nothing was touched." She glanced at him and smiled. "Thanks for fixing it again."

"Good idea." He smiled. "And you're welcome."

He was kind of pissed for not having thought of it himself. It just proved when he was personally involved in any case, it would throw him off his game. And he was in this deep, in two different ways—what with avoiding a murder charge, plus, not letting Anna get shot or worse. At the compound they had everything running through video cameras at over a dozen locations. Somebody was always going through them, making sure nothing happened they needed to know about. He should have done the same as soon as they arrived home from the police station.

"I saw him."

She raised her head and studied him. "You saw who?" she asked cautiously.

"Brendan. He was the one driving the big truck."

She bolted to her feet and threw her arms around Flynn.

He hugged her close. "I'm so sorry," she said, her voice muffled by his shirt.

"I am too, but at the same time, I'm relieved. We have the right bad guy. There's no one else out there doing this to us."

"Did the cop see him?"

"The first cop was there with me. The second took off after him. The one seemed to think they'd have no trouble catching Brendan in a roadblock. But I highly doubt it. Chances are he's already long gone."

She pulled back and stared up at him in horror. "Really?"

He nodded.

Just then the doorbell rang. She clung to him instead of stepping away so he could answer.

"Maybe it's Logan."

She gave him a questioning look but pulled back, following him. He opened the door with her standing right behind him.

Sure enough it was Logan.

And he was bearing gifts.

The smell of pizza filled the hallway. She laughed. "Perfect timing. I'm starving again."

He handed her the pizzas and she took them into the kitchen. Thank God he was okay. She had no idea if he just ran off to get the food and hadn't told them, meaning for it to be a surprise, or if something else happened. She brought out plates and poured Logan a cup of coffee, topped hers off, and filled Flynn's also.

Still talking, the men came into the kitchen, laughing and joking.

"I guess he didn't see it then?" Anna asked.

Flynn shook his head. "He followed us just out to the freeway, but since I took the most direct way home to miss all the irritating lights, he actually went into town and ordered pizza."

"Then that was a very slow delivery," she muttered. "We parted ways over an hour ago."

"True enough," Logan said. "But I also stopped at the liquor store and picked up some beer. I figured Flynn could use a little bit of downtime on that whole stress-level thing."

Flynn grabbed a beer, popping off the top. "You're damn right I could. You haven't heard the latest."

When Flynn filled him in, Logan stared at him, his jaw dropping. "You're saying that, if I'd followed behind you, I would have seen the goddamn asshole? Might've been able to run his plates?"

"Yeah. Instead the police are chasing him down. But I highly doubt they'll catch him."

"Hell, Brendan was in the same evasive driving-maneuver training we were. He'll shake that off easily."

Flynn nodded. "I know. I'm expecting him to return. Possibly tonight."

HE EXPECTED SOME kind of response from Anna. When there was none, he turned to study her face. It was white, like ice that had set too long in a freezer. He reached across and grabbed her hands. "I don't want you lulled into thinking this is over. Brendan's actions have escalated. There's almost no time between his various little attacks now. He'll come for the jugular, and we're ready."

She stared back at him mutely.

He squeezed her fingers and reassured her. "Remember,

this is what we do."

She shook her head. "It's what *you* do, not me."

"And that's fine. You just have to trust us."

Logan chimed in. "We have to be on alert and prepared for an attack."

"What kind of an attack?"

"That's the big question. Your security system is back up and running, which is good. But we can't count on that. He took it out the first time. He'll do it again. I did set an alarm for that eventuality. So if the system goes offline, an alarm will sound," Flynn said.

"You can do that?"

"Absolutely. Security systems are way too easy to knock out."

"So we just sit here and wait?" Her voice rose at the end. She pulled her hands free and reached up, giving her face a good scrub. "This is just too unbelievable."

"I think Katina would say that same thing. She went through hell too."

Anna shook her head. "Sure, but she'd seen and done something. I haven't and the animals don't deserve this."

"It doesn't matter who deserves it. This is what's happening, it's what's on the table right now. Don't compare the situation to anyone or anything else. We have to deal with what we have to deal with." Logan's voice was hard. Determined.

Flynn agreed. But he also knew Anna didn't live in the same world they did. Cloak-and-dagger stuff was foreign to her. She dealt with puppies and kittens, and her biggest problem was paying vet bills and getting enough food to feed the animals she looked after. A far cry from his world.

On the other hand, it was a good balance. He saw the

world in a much nicer light when he was around her. Sure, people were often assholes to animals, and for those he'd cheerfully take them out in a dark alley and give them a lesson about how hard the world could really be. But Anna was all heart. She'd spent her life saving animals. She just needed a hand. And as he considered her words from earlier, maybe a move wasn't a bad idea. A little farther out of town would be good. He could see the neighbors not being impressed when she was full with thirty or forty barking dogs. There had to be noise ordinances. She had a business license, but if the city officials ever found a reason to cancel that, or change the scope of the license, he figured they would do it in a heartbeat.

Particularly after this session, her place would be deemed trouble. It wasn't her fault; but his. And for that he was terribly sorry. However, the only thing he could do was get her through this and keep her alive.

Chapter 14

A FTER FINISHING A piece of pizza, she picked up her coffee and walked to her office. "I'll update the website for the other two dogs. See if we can get some interest on Jimbo and his buddy, Duggy."

In truth, she just wanted to return to something resembling a normal life. She turned on her computer and brought up the website. She quickly made the changes, then put Jimbo and Duggy's photos up front and center. She lowered the adoption fee, hoping to trigger some interest from anybody. As soon as she was done, she reached for the phone and called the Rabbit Rescue. She'd been hoping to hand off her rabbit to someone as a family pet. But after a certain number of days, it wasn't fair to keep him in the cage. He'd be much better off at the rescue. There were many acres of land so the rabbits were free to run, and the food was supplemented.

She knew they wouldn't be open at this hour, but she could leave a message. Knowing it was a small business like hers, she was surprised when somebody answered. She explained who she was and what she had.

"My husband's actually in town right now. You want him to run by and pick him up?"

Anna gasped in surprise. "Yes, that would be lovely. Thank you. By the way, do you happen to know anybody who would want a hamster?" she asked in a half-joking manner.

"Well, my daughter is looking for one. I'll tell my husband to take a look while he's there."

At the end of that very happy phone call, Anna got up from her chair and raced out to the kitchen where the men were having a conversation. "Hey, Flynn. A man'll be coming by to pick up the rabbit. He runs a big rabbit rescue outside of town. They're happy to take him."

"Nice. I'm sure the rabbit would much prefer to be free than in a cage."

"I don't know why I didn't think of it earlier," she said. "I was trying to find a family for him, but you're right, free is better."

"It's definitely better," Logan said.

"Also, he'll take a look at the hamster for his daughter."

"So it's possible that, after tonight, it would be down to the two dogs?"

She stared at him in wonder. "Plus, the snake and four cats."

He laughed. "Four is not bad."

Logan laughed too. "I better not tell my dad that you've got cats here. He's quite a feline lover."

She rounded on him. "Tell him. Tell him. Maybe he'll take one or two."

"What's the deal here with the animals anyway?"

She explained how she got them all fixed and kept trying to find homes for them.

"But when you have no animals, then what?"

"I'm wondering if I should sell and move the shelter somewhere else. A place where the dogs would have more room." She winced. "I can't exactly say I'm terribly happy here after Jonas's murder. It doesn't feel like home anymore."

"It's not a bad idea. But a move like that will cost money."

"I know. But the property values here have gone up, and if I move out of town, I might be able to get into a better financial position."

"Did you say this place is paid for?"

She nodded. "That is the one good thing. But all the pens would need to be moved or rebuilt. I'd need a place like this, but better. I'd have to find something within my budget."

The two men looked at each other. She walked to the coffeepot and filled her cup. Money was such a pain in her existence. It wasn't fair. All she wanted to do was to save animals.

She stared out the back. "I'm thinking of bringing the rabbit and hamster inside. I do have traveling cages for them."

On that note, she put down her cup and headed outside. She quickly shifted the rabbit into her arms, giving him a heartfelt cuddle, loving its soft texture and gentle personality. Then she moved him into a smaller cage and gave him a few little treats. The hamster was still in a big cage, and she thought the whole cage could just go with him. She picked both up and carried them in the kitchen, setting them on the table beside the men. "I need to find a home for the snake too."

Logan looked at her with interest. "You have a snake?"

She nodded. "He really should go to a reptile rescue."

"Is there one in Houston?"

"I don't know. I haven't had a chance to look. I just got

him the day before Jonas was killed."

"That's right. He wasn't here when I was, was he?"

She shook her head. "No." She glanced down at the rabbit and hamster. "But with all the successive moving of animals, I'm thinking maybe the snake—with its big slow-healing back injury—would be in a much better place at the reptile rescue."

She gave the men a bright smile, grabbed her coffee and said, "I'll go take a look."

She walked back to her office. She didn't know what had happened to the snake—the first she had had here—but if it had been somebody's pet, she'd want to make sure it went to a better home this time. And a reptile rescue might be the best place for it. If she was lucky enough to have one close by.

She made several phone calls, realizing she was pushing the limit for her good luck, but it was hard to let go of an idea once she sunk her teeth into it.

Her research paid off. She found a reptile rescue and several reptile clubs, and they often kept unwanted animals. She found a couple email addresses and darted off emails, sending a description and photos of the snake.

She'd be hesitant to take in reptiles again without having any idea what to do with them. They would be hard to sell to families. Still, if she could find a place for one or knew who to call when she was given another, that was a different story.

Satisfied she'd done what she could, she stood up just as the front doorbell rang. That should be the man for the rabbit. As she walked to the front door, she found both men waiting on her. Logan was in the corner of the living room. Flynn stood at her side as she opened the door to find a middle-aged man smiling down at her.

"I hear there's a rabbit and hamster."

She welcomed him inside and led the way back to the kitchen. "I've had the rabbit for a couple weeks. It's time for him to find a better place. I haven't had any luck getting him adopted."

"It's one of the reasons we set up the rescue. So often they are just released and become dog food."

She gave him a long look. "I know. It's so hard." She motioned at the big rabbit. "There he is, and he's very healthy."

"Perfect." The man looked over at the hamster and smiled. "Apparently I know a little girl looking for one." Because he was taking the rabbit off her hands to put him in the rescue, there'd be no money exchanged. She smiled. "Well, outside of the hamster's vet fees, he hasn't cost very much, so if you just want to take him for your daughter, I'm happy with that."

The man looked at her, a question in his eyes. "You don't have adoption fees?"

She nodded. "Usually, but hamsters aren't very much to handle anyway."

He pulled out his wallet and gave her twenty bucks. "Buy a bag of dog food."

She accepted it gratefully. "You want a receipt?"

He shook his head. "Not an issue. You okay with me keeping the cages?"

She nodded. "Yes. Thanks for looking after the rabbit. We need more rescues in this world."

He carried both pets out the front door. The whole transaction had taken less than twenty minutes. She'd moved out two more animals. As soon as he got in the vehicle and drove away, she turned to walk back toward the house, Flynn at her side.

"That's two more animals getting homes."

"You've had a great day," Flynn admitted. "I'm so happy for you."

She grinned. She wanted to throw her arms around him, but instead hooked her arm through his and said, "I'm delighted."

He put his foot on the first step, and she jumped quickly onto the step above, intent on turning to give him a quick kiss, when an odd sound came and a harsh burn ran across her arm. She cried out in pain. What just happened?

"Stay down."

She had no intention of going anywhere. But now her arm stung something awful. Lifting her hand, which hid the extent of the wound, she studied it, cataloguing what had just happened. The huge black truck that had tried to run them off the road drove past the house, the driver holding a handgun and spraying gunfire onto the property.

She cried out in shock as bullets rained over them. She crunched up into as small a ball as she could. Dimly in the background, she heard Flynn call out, "Look after Anna."

The big truck roared, its brakes squealing when it picked up speed as it went around the corner. Then a second vehicle raced behind.

Just as suddenly as it had begun, there was silence.

She lay on the porch, controlling her breathing and the urge to scream.

"Are you okay, Anna?"

She turned toward Logan's voice behind her head. He was just inside the house. In a daze she answered, "I think so. Is he gone?"

"Yes, and Flynn went after him."

With Logan's help, she made it into a sitting position. She gasped when he touched her arm.

"You shot?"

She shook her head. "I don't think so."

Up on her feet and inside the kitchen, she stumbled to the table and sat down heavily. With the light she saw blood streaming between her fingers, dripping down her arm. And of course, the minute she saw it, she felt faint. And then the pain hit. She lowered her head to the table and focused on deep breaths. She didn't think the bullet had gone through, but had no way of knowing because she couldn't even see her hand.

"Let me take a look," Logan said.

This will hurt like crap.

He gently peeled away her fingers and put a cool washcloth over the wound. He put firm pressure on it, making her cry out.

"It's bleeding pretty badly. I have to clean it up a bit to see just how bad it is."

"How bad? I presume I'm going to the hospital." She stared out the window at the animals. "The cats and two dogs. Can you handle them?"

"Sure can," he said cheerfully. "Though the priority isn't the animals, but getting you to the hospital."

"True enough, but they have to be scared. There has been an awful lot of noise here. This is not the environment I wanted for any of them."

"And it's not likely to ever happen again. Once we get this resolved, you can go back to that nice peaceful way of living."

"And why is it that it sounded like *boring* was the next

adjective you would use?"

He laughed. "Flynn took the big truck," he said. "You okay if I drive your car?"

She nodded. "Not a whole lot of options."

"Not unless you want to pay for an ambulance."

She snorted. "Not only am I not paying for one, but it's nowhere near bad enough for it. I can probably drive myself, if you want to stay here and look after the animals for me," she said hopefully.

"Not happening. I suspect Flynn will be back fairly soon, and he can look after them."

She had to be happy with that because no way would Logan budge. With her hand again holding the washcloth firm on her arm, Logan reached for her purse, then tucked it over her other shoulder. Afterward he grabbed up her keys, turned out the lights, reset the security and got her to her car in a minute flat. He gently helped her into the passenger side, buckled her in and jogged around to the driver's side.

"You don't have to treat me like an invalid. I won't break."

"But we don't know how long that will hold because right now, you're leaking."

She looked at him, startled, then burst out laughing.

With a big grin on his face, obviously happy he had shifted her mood, he drove her straight to the nearest emergency room.

As he drove, she asked, "It was the same truck, wasn't it?"

He nodded. "Flynn and I recognized the driver. It was Brendan for sure."

"He's really not going stop until Flynn is shot, is he?"

Logan glanced over at her sideways. "And even then he's not likely to. He's quite fixated on Flynn. Chances are it'll end up with somebody getting killed."

"As long as it's not Flynn."

"Agreed. But I don't want to see you or any of the rest of us hurt either."

She shook her head. "No, that wouldn't be very nice." She stared out the window, a real deep hatred burning inside her for the man completely destroying her life. "I hope Flynn catches and beats the crap out of him."

"You can be guaranteed that we will catch him. If it's not today, it'll be tomorrow."

"He has to be stopped before he hurts anybody else. He just has to." She couldn't live with anything else.

NO WAY IN hell would he let Brendan get away with this. He'd heard Anna's cry of pain and knew she'd been hit. He'd checked it quickly, found it wasn't bad, then raced for the truck. But after that round of bullets hitting the house, he couldn't be sure. He knew Logan would look after her. What Flynn had to do was get this asshole and run him down. Somehow. They had to put a stop to this forever.

Brendan had a head start. Moving around a street corner, Flynn caught sight of the truck several blocks ahead. He picked up speed, catching the light just before it turned red. Then gave chase. The cops would be after both of them. An APB should already be out on Brendan's truck from the last one. He couldn't believe the cops didn't catch him, but then, like Logan said, Brendan had been damn good. It was going be hard to stop him. If Flynn could follow Brendan someplace, see where he was roosting, that would be a different story.

Still a block behind, he watched as Brendan made a sharp left. He followed and watched Brendan take another turn into an alleyway.

That could be good or bad. He drove past it to see what Brendan was doing and saw the truck taking a turn about halfway down, into what appeared to be a backyard.

Flynn quickly pulled off to the side, turned off the engine and lights, and ran on foot down the alleyway. If he could at least find the truck, he would know where Brendan had gone to ground. At the halfway point he slowed, studying each property as he went. These were run-down houses. He'd have to say it was more of a shady area of town from the looks of the backyards, but it could just be a poor one. As he came to an open road, he saw a truck parked halfway in, and it looked like the one Brendan had driven. As he sorted things out, he saw Brendan busy throwing stuff into the back of it.

Flynn stopped and considered his options. It would be stupid to go in without backup, but no way could he afford to lose track of Brendan. Flynn stepped back and pulled out his phone, quickly texting Levi this location. Flynn only had a general guess as to the street he was on. He clicked on his phone's GPS and sent the coordinates to Levi as well.

Still huddled in the alley keeping an eye on Brendan, he sent the next text to Logan. When there was no answer, he frowned. He didn't know how bad things were at home, but he could only hope this wouldn't be something he'd regret.

Levi sent back a confirmation.

Stay there out of sight. Cops are on their way.

He stared down at the message and wondered if that was a good or bad thing. Because if they came in with guns blazing, Brendan would be out of here. And no way would Flynn be able to stop the truck on foot.

Brendan walked to the back of the house. If Flynn could disable the truck, Brendan would be stuck on foot, and it would be a whole lot easier to catch him.

The backyard was a wide open grassy area, and the truck offered no cover. As he studied the neighboring houses, he saw the closest one offered privacy with their fenced yard. He creeped over the back gate of the neighbor's yard to where he could jump the fence close to the truck. He listened carefully and peered through but saw no sign of anyone. Gathering his strength, in one smooth movement he cleared the fence, landing softly on the other side.

He pulled out his knife and stuck it into the tire on the rear right side, then moved to the left and did the same. At least now Brendan couldn't use this vehicle to get away. Inside the garage was a small car. But without moving the truck, no way could he get the car out either. Flynn crept to the front of the truck and stabbed the front tires as well. He stood up to take a look inside the front seat. It looked like Brendan had packed for a long trip.

If he opened the truck door, it would likely sound an alarm, turn on the lights, and all that would alert Brendan. As Flynn peered into the back, he saw duffel bags, several of them. As if Brendan was heading out of town for good. Or at least until he could formulate his next plan of attack.

Well, good luck with that. Flynn planned to have this one locked down before Brendan could make another move.

The back door of the house slammed. Flynn had no

place to hide. There was just enough room between the garage and the neighbor's fence to squeeze behind it. Brendan threw another bag into the back of the truck, then stopped and stared. And then he started swearing.

"Jesus Christ, what the hell happened to my tires?" He turned and glared around the yard, searching for the culprit. He ran inside the garage, then down the alley. Finally, he walked back toward the vehicle, shouting obscenities.

Flynn was about to stand up, only to realize the jam he was in. He didn't have any way to sneak up on Brendan. As he opened the truck door, pulling out his bags, Flynn came behind Brendan, grabbed him by the neck and slammed his head into the side of the door. Brendan dropped and rolled, his legs kicking, catching Flynn, and down he went. Brendan was on him in an instant, his hands latched around Flynn's throat.

Flynn tucked his knees up, caught Brendan in the groin while reaching up to press his eyeballs deep into his skull. Brendan roared. But they'd both been trained with military tactics, and it was a fair fight.

Only Flynn had a little more at stake–Anna.

The thought of her bleeding right now was enough to keep Flynn punching and kicking wildly. In the background he dimly heard sirens filling the air. Suddenly, Brendan was hauled off Flynn and held down to the ground.

Guns were pointed at Flynn. He raised his hand and said, "I'm Flynn. He's the shooter."

The cops didn't believe him. "Roll over on your belly with your hands straight out in front of you."

He complied. This would be sorted out with time. The best thing he could do was comply. All he could think about at the moment was that they caught Brendan. Thank God, they'd actually gotten him.

Now to tell Anna so she could rest easy too.

Chapter 15

"ANY WORD FROM Flynn?" Anna asked as she sat on the hard bed in the emergency room.

They were waiting for the doctor to arrive. Logan had told the nurse how Anna had been shot, so she suspected it wouldn't be all that long to get medical attention. On the other hand, this was a big city. Shootings happened almost every single day. She was now a statistic.

"He texted to say he'd run Brendan down to a house. Cops were on the way, and Levi already knew." Logan pulled out his phone. "But there's been nothing since."

"Maybe you can contact Levi and see if he knows anything more."

"Already in progress." Logan nodded, his fingers busy on his phone.

When Logan was finished, he sat back and studied her. "You still don't have any color in your face. How are you feeling?"

"Shaky." She gave him a wan smile. "When we know where Flynn is, I'll feel better."

Just then the doctor came in. "What's this I hear about you being shot, young lady?"

"Shot at," she corrected. "Actually, I have no idea how bad it is."

"Let's take a look."

And he did, poking and prodding. It hurt. She had tears running down her cheeks; she couldn't hold them back. Logan walked to the curtain and stared out toward the waiting room. She figured it was to give her a moment of privacy. All she really wanted to do was curl up on the pillow and bawl.

When the doctor was done, he said, "It could be much worse. The bullet went through the fleshy part of the arm."

She stared at him. "Pardon?" She stared down at her arm but couldn't see anything. "I didn't think I had a fleshy part of my arm," she said in disgust.

The doctor grinned. "Sometimes it's an advantage not being a pure bone rack."

From near the curtain, she could hear Logan snigger.

"Yeah, sure, you're having fun with this. Now you can go tell everybody I'm so fat that the bullet couldn't miss me," she joked.

"I never would," he said. "Besides, the last thing you are is fat. You could easily use another ten pounds."

"I could not. I'm just fine the way I am." She appealed to the doctor beside her. "Right, Doc?"

"I'm not getting in the middle of this one."

She glared at Logan. "See? He agreed with me."

Logan opened his mouth to retort and then snapped it closed and shook his head. "I'll put your lack of logic down to you being injured. Obviously it's a handicap."

She glared at the doctor and said, "You didn't actually tell me how bad it is."

"Nope, I didn't. It'll need some stitches and cleaning. It will be a few days before you can use it at all."

She looked at him in shock. "You know it's my right arm, correct?"

"You know how many people I get through here who tell me something similar?" He picked up his tablet and started to walk away, adding, "I'll send the nurse back in to clean it. Then I'll return to stitch you up."

"I guess that means I'll be here for a while?"

Logan nodded. "I'll step out to make some phone calls." He turned to look back at her and asked, "Will you be okay?"

She waved him off. "I'll be fine. Go find out where Flynn and Brendan are."

When he was gone, the nurse came in. Anna was very grateful Logan wasn't here because she became a blubbering baby. She kept apologizing to the nurse.

The nurse said, "Just relax as much as you can."

Finally the nurse was done. Wiping back her tears, Anna asked, "Can I lie down now?"

In fact, the nurse helped her to lie flat. "I'll give you a shot so when the doctor comes and puts in the stitches, you won't feel it."

"Will it hurt?" She was feeling like a baby. This was so not like her. But then she couldn't remember the last time she'd had any kind of physical trauma. And she would blame as much of this on shock as she could. She felt really woozy too. The pain for the last half hour made her body ache. And she was chilled.

The pain of the needle wouldn't be as bad as cleaning the wound had. The nurse reached down and touched her forehead. "Are you cold?"

Anna nodded, and her teeth started chattering. "It just hit all of a sudden."

"I'll get you a warm blanket. You just lie here and rest."

The nurse took off her gloves, tossed them in the garbage and disappeared. Anna rolled over so her injured arm was higher than her legs and curled up into a ball. And then the tears poured. They were so damn hard to stop. By the time the nurse came back, Anna was shaking from the cold. A warm blanket was draped over her shivering form.

The nurse whispered, "Take it easy. You'll be fine now. This is just shock. Give yourself a few minutes to adjust." Then she was gone again.

Finally her tears stopped, and the shivering calmed down. And warm once again, Anna closed her eyes and drifted off to sleep.

She was awakened rather rudely when the doctor came in and asked in a bright, cheerful voice, "You ready for those stitches now?"

She stared up at him and shook her head. "Is anybody ever ready for them?"

He gave her a quiet smile. "Well, the alternative would be much worse. Let's get this sewn up."

She lay quietly in that position while he went ahead and did what he needed to. Thankfully, it was just a few tugs. Nothing bad.

When he was done, he said, "I'll write a prescription for some pain medication. You need to see your doctor in ten days. If you have any sharp pain, pus from the site, red lines running up and down your arm, or any kind of problem, you get to your doctor immediately. Better yet, come straight back to Emergency." He waited until she looked him directly in the eye before he added, "Do you hear me?"

She nodded. "I hear you."

"I'll make sure she's fine," Logan said from the doorway.

The doctor looked at him. "Are you her boyfriend?"

"No, a good friend."

Logan stepped closer. "Her boyfriend went after the asshole who did this to her."

The doctor nodded. "Good. I presume I will have another body in need of repair soon enough." He handed the prescription to Logan, walked out, calling back, "Glad she has someone looking after her. We all need that."

Logan studied Anna's face as she still lay under the blanket. "Do you need to stay overnight? I might be able to arrange that."

She shook her head. "No, I'll be fine." She looked up at him. "But it's awfully hard to move."

He gently pulled back the blanket and held out his arms. She grabbed him with her good arm and slowly leveraged herself to a sitting position.

Just then the nurse came bustling back in. "Oh, good, you're up. I came to bring you a sling. Keep the arm elevated to take the pressure off the joints, and don't use it for several days. Do you understand?"

At this point Anna found it easier to nod at every instruction. She'd do what she had to, and do the best she could. But honestly, how could she possibly not use her main arm? That would be damn near impossible.

Thankfully, the bullet hadn't hit a bone or artery, and it was a small injury compared to having a bullet tear through her organs. This was an inconvenience, but she would live with it.

It could have been a lot worse.

FLYNN CALLED ANNA. No answer. Had they remembered to grab her phone before they raced to the hospital? He could only presume that's where they were. It was where he'd have taken her. But since she wasn't answering her cell phone...

Quickly he dialed the number to the shelter and got the answering machine. Next he called Logan.

"She's fine," Logan said. "The bullet went through the soft tissue of her arm. She's got stitches, and it's bandaged. We're just heading to her car to drive home."

"Oh, thank God." Flynn pinched the bridge of his nose as he gave a silent prayer of thanks. "When I ran out like that, after the second barrage of bullets, I wasn't sure how badly hurt she was. I was just about to race to the hospital now to see if she was still there."

"We have to pick up a prescription, and that'll take at least ten minutes, so we should be home in half an hour. She's tired, still a little in shock, but fine and in fighting form, evidenced by the fact that she wouldn't stay in the hospital any longer."

"No, I don't think she likes hospitals." He could be wrong, but he didn't think so.

"I don't think anybody does. Anyway, can you meet us at her house? I want to get her into the vehicle and moving as fast as possible. She's looking a little on the pale side." Logan sighed.

In the background, Flynn could hear her snapping, "No, I'm not. Tell him I'm fine. He'll just worry."

And that—more than anything—made Flynn feel so much better. If she was in a feisty mood, then she was doing just fine. "I'll be home as soon as I can," he said. "The police have Brendan in custody. But I'm hanging here just in case they need me. I don't want the cops to come back to the place tonight. She's been through enough."

"This isn't your fault. Think forward."

When he ended the call, Flynn turned to study the area.

The cops were all over the place. Then again, this guy had been in several cop chases, and was a suspect of a drive-by shooting and murder. There should be a lot of attention to this property, the vehicle, and Brendan himself. Flynn wanted to go down to the police station and beat the shit out of Brendan to get some answers. But Flynn knew that wouldn't go down well. He walked over to a cop and asked, "Do you need me here?"

The cop studied him. "I want your statement. Give me a brief version now, and you can go down to the station later."

It took a little bit, but when he finally got through it all, the cop with his notepad said, "Okay, see you at the station tomorrow morning. We'll go through this place with a finetooth comb. We need proof he's the one who killed Jonas, and it would be nice to have proof he's the one responsible for the drive-by shooting and the attack on Anna."

That set up several more questions in Flynn's mind. By the time he was done and free to go, another half hour had passed. A half hour that really didn't matter because now he knew Brendan was caught and life could return to normal. They needed as much evidence as they could possibly get to pin it all on Brendan. Flynn didn't want to see the asshole get out for thirty plus years.

A part of him wanted to see Brendan go out in a blaze of gunfire so Flynn wouldn't have to worry about him any-more. But now that he was in police custody, Flynn was pretty sure they were in for a long-drawn-out court case. As long as Brendan didn't get a chance to be released on bail, then Flynn was good with that.

Speaking of which, he called Levi. "I guess there is no

way we can stop Brendan from getting released on bail, is there? Not with murder charges against him, right?"

"Only if they can pin it on him," Levi said. "If he's cooperative and agrees to stay around, they may release him without bail. If they have evidence worth charging him with murder or attempted murder, they could still release him if he posts bail. Otherwise, they can hold him for twenty-four hours without charging him."

"We can't let him get bail," Flynn said. "I know his brother is local, but Brendan is a newcomer to this area, unemployed."

"Good point. I'll make a phone call to the DA. He owes us after last time. Maybe he can use his clout to influence bail."

Flynn had forgotten about Rhodes's problem with Sienna and the DA. Rhodes had saved the DA's life. It was always good to have friends in high places, especially to have them in cases like this. It was pretty major. It wasn't as if Flynn wanted anything illegal done, but if there were doors that could be closed, he didn't want Brendan getting out. If he came back after Flynn, it would be bad. But it was Anna who kept getting hurt. And that could not be allowed to continue.

By the time he made it to his truck and back out to the main road, driving toward Anna's place, he could feel some of his adrenaline draining away. It was amazing how good it was, keeping you going when everything was busy. But once that adrenaline shot drained out, it left you pretty empty.

He hoped some pizza was still left. He'd have some of that when he got there. But he knew the animals might be feeling the stress of these events too. Maybe tonight they all could finally get a good night's sleep for the first time in days.

As he pulled up into the driveway, Anna's car was already there. Which was a good thing. He hopped out, locked up the truck and walked to the front door. The security system was set. He punched in the code to let himself in the front door and called out, "Anna, you home?"

He closed the door, reset the alarm and turned to see Logan standing in the living room. A finger to his lips.

"She's just fallen asleep on the couch."

Flynn took a look. Sure enough, she was curled up with a pillow under her head and a blanket across her shoulders. Sleeping. But her face was pale, waxy. He leaned down and kissed her cheek gently and whispered, "I'm sorry. But it's all over now. You're safe."

She didn't shift, and he realized that, between the pain medication and stress, she was out cold. He turned back toward Logan. "You probably should have taken her to her bed before she crashed."

"I tried," Logan said. "But she was a mite too stubborn. She wanted to be down here when you came back."

"Like that'll help. Now I have to carry her upstairs," he joked.

"And you won't have a problem doing that," Logan said comfortably. "Chances are you'll stay in the bedroom beside her."

Flynn glanced back at her and said in a low voice, "I'd like nothing better."

"I'm damn glad they caught Brendan." Logan shook his head. "I wondered what it would take to bring down that asshole."

"And I'm still not sure he'll stay down. There's just too many ways he could get off. What if they don't have enough evidence to pin the murder on him? We can't prove it was a drive-by shooting if there are no eyewitness reports seeing the truck or him. It would be my word against his. There's just so much circumstantial evidence. And the fact that he has a brother close and he's ex-military too, a soft judge could let him go while they collect more evidence."

"What? Surely not."

Flynn shrugged. He turned a tired face toward Logan and said, "You and Levi both know it can happen. You've seen all kinds things occur in the courts. Honestly, I'd rather the guy was dead. But that's out of my hands."

"Make sure it's not by your hands," Logan warned. "It's tough in our business. We've had to kill. But we can't make it a choice to do so."

"I hear you. It doesn't mean I don't want to." He cast one more look at Anna. "I'd pound the shit right out of him if I could get my hands on him for what he did to Anna alone." He walked into the kitchen. "Any pizza left?"

"God, I hope so. I know there's beer."

Within minutes the two men sat down to warmed-up pizza and cold beer. Flynn stretched out his legs with a happy sigh after three pieces. He took a long swig of beer and said, "Goddamn, am I glad it's over with."

Logan nodded. "Do you think it's safe to leave you two alone tonight?"

Flynn gave his buddy a lopsided grin. "If she wasn't injured, I'd say get the hell out of here, but with her sleeping like she is, injured the way she was..." He shook his head. "It'll be sleep tonight."

Logan gave a good-natured laugh. "Understood. I'm really surprised, though I shouldn't be, as I'd heard about the two of you. But now that I see you together, I'm happy for you. You're really well-matched."

Flynn shrugged. "I'm not sure what that means anymore. But I know I found someone very special, and I want to hang on to her."

"Good. Then you won't do anything stupid. I doubt she'll be rushed into anything she's not ready for."

"No, but it's time for a change for her. She's contemplating selling and moving a little out of town. She's hoping she'll get more land for the animals. Then go bigger for the rescues. But that depends on all kinds of things, including money." He reached out with his beer bottle and tapped Logan's. "Your dad did a good thing with that check."

Logan's eyebrows shot up. "He sent one?"

Flynn nodded. "I saw the company name on it. She needed that money."

"Well, the old man's got it, and he donates hundreds of thousands a year to charities. There's no reason some of it can't filter here."

"That's a great way to look at it."

As Flynn finished his beer, he stood up and put his empty back into the case, grabbing another. As he did so, he heard an odd sound. He froze, turned and looked out to the backyard. The two dogs were in the pen; they needed to be brought into their cages. And it was already damn late. But he knew how Anna would worry. Yet he couldn't see what caused that sound. Still suspicious, he knew how easily normal night noises could be scary. "There are four cats and two dogs left to look after. I better get out there."

"Let me give you a hand."

Leaving the beer behind, the two walked out the back door. He led Jimbo and Duggy inside to their cages, gave them fresh water and food and both got a hug. They walked to the cats, made short work of the litter box, and with Logan's help, dumped out a couple cans of cat food and gave them fresh water. He looked down the long rows of cages and said, "It's the least animals she's ever had."

"Well, there's certainly a need for her to do more. But after this crap..." Logan shook his head. "You're right. Maybe moving would be better."

"It'll be hard to recover from it here. I can't imagine too many charities will want to donate with all the bad publicity that'll hit the papers. I'd like to be wrong, bu ..."

"I could ask my dad to give a hand. Not so much with donating more money because I don't know what he's doing with that, but he could surely put out a good word. Also, she's got prime real estate here. Maybe she should move. If she can afford to, this is the best time because she doesn't have many animals. We can get the whole gang to give her a hand one day, get it done fast and simple."

"Do you think the guys would mind?"

Logan snorted. "You know how they love to be over the top, do it all at once and better than anyone else. They'd die for her, particularly if she's to be your ladylove." Logan waggled his eyebrows.

Flynn smiled. "I guess that's what families are all about."

Logan slapped him on the shoulder. "Remember you're part of the team now. You're one of us again. You are not out in the cold anymore."

Flynn glanced at Logan once more and smiled. "With

you, buddy, I never have been. Thanks for always being there."

"That's what friends are for."

Chapter 16

ANNA WOKE TO a silence that was deep and unnerving. It took a long moment to figure out exactly where she was and why she was on her couch with a blanket over her. As soon as she jolted to a sitting position, she remembered. The pain in her arm kicked in. She leaned back and took several deep breaths, waiting for the throbbing to calm down. Her arm was in a sling, but some of that support had shifted. The bandage was solid and should do for the night. It was definitely dark out. And it sounded like she was alone. She got to her feet, made her way to the downstairs bathroom, used the facilities and washed her hands. She stared at her face in the mirror and saw drops of dried blood, her ashen complexion, and the great big bags under her eyes. "Wow, a beauty you are not."

With her left hand she awkwardly grabbed a washcloth, wet it and did a half-assed effort to wipe her face clean. She wasn't sure how the blood got up there. No way could she manage a shower tonight. She wasn't sure why she had awakened. That was one of the reasons she hated drugs as much as they did her. They never worked as well or as long as they should.

She opened the bathroom door and stepped out. Lights were on in the kitchen, but no sound came from there. As she walked into the brightly lit room, she noticed that half a pizza was gone, and several more beer bottles, opened and emptied, were on the table. So the guys were either out front at the vehicles or in back with the animals.

Dear God, she hadn't brought the dogs in. She opened the door and listened. But she couldn't hear anything. She wanted to call the dogs, but she'd been through enough scary shit lately and didn't want to bring any attention to herself. Then she heard voices, laughter and a door shutting. She sank back against the doorjamb, relieved, closing her eyelids as she realized Flynn and Logan were in with the cats. Her phone buzzed. She glanced at it and got her second good news of the day. The reptile center had room for her snake. She would contact them to arrange for the transfer.

She beamed at the guys as they walked toward her. "Thank you for looking after the animals. The snake has a new home as soon as I can make it happen."

"That's great news," Logan said.

"What the hell are you doing up and outside?" Flynn snapped. "You're injured. You should be back in bed—your own, not on the couch."

"Thank you, Flynn. How are you, Flynn? It's so nice of you to be concerned about my condition, Flynn. But please take it upon yourself to be anything but an asshole."

Logan howled with laughter. "Oh, my God, you two are so perfect for each other."

Both Flynn and Anna turned to glare at Logan. He snickered, but it subsided. Flynn motioned to her. She turned around and went back into the house. She decided she would follow his silent command because she felt tired enough that she needed to go sit down again, not because he told her to. She found a chair she assumed they hadn't been using at the kitchen table and collapsed into it. She eyed the pizza, wondering if she wanted a piece.

"You want some?" Logan asked, his gaze following hers.

She smiled. "Would you mind putting it in the microwave for a few seconds for me?"

"Not at all." He picked up two slices from the two different boxes, plunked them on a plate and popped it in the microwave.

She sat back as the aroma of pizza filled the room.

Flynn asked, "You want a beer? Although it's probably not a good idea with the painkillers."

"I'm not much of a beer drinker anyway. Thanks. Now if there was tea …"

Logan hit the button on the teakettle as he brought her the pizza. "Hot water coming up."

She stared down at the pizza, smiled brightly and said, "Thank you. Nice to know you're housetrained."

He chuckled. "I am. I don't know about this guy though."

She turned sideways, glancing at Flynn. "He's got more of the junkyard dog thing going on."

Logan howled again.

Flynn glared at him. "Enough already. Shut the hell up."

Logan subsided slightly, but his eyes twinkled as he looked from one to the other. "I guess now that you're safe, I can go home to my own house?"

"Do you have your own?" Anna asked in interest. "I thought you lived at the compound."

"I do. And my father is close by. He has a huge house with my own suite of rooms in it." He gave her a sheepish grin. "Seems silly to buy my own when he's got an apartment for me, plus, I do live at the compound."

"Nice, no bills anywhere." She shook her head. "Damn nice."

He laughed. "There is just my father and me," he said. "I don't really want to move out and lose the relationship we have."

"I wouldn't either," she said softly. "If you have any relationship that you care about, you do what you need to nurture it."

"My thoughts exactly. Besides, I'm never around to look after a place, so thankfully people at both locations take care of things for me." He grinned. "And I'm a lousy cook."

"But you have Alfred. I would love to have an Alfred of my own," she said in a wistful tone. "My God, he's perfect. He does all the organizing, looking after the house. He cooks. He cleans…" She shook her head. "We should all have an Alfred."

"No argument there."

Flynn looked over at Logan. "Your dad has several Alfreds. And our counterpart in Africa, Bullard, has Dave, who's damn near a clone of Alfred. And in England, one of our friends we stay with, Charles, has a second Alfred clone. There's just something about that type of gentleman."

"*Gentleman.* Yes, Alfred's very much that. He's almost like an old butler."

"The compound does have staff members who come and handle things. It's well over 25,000 square feet. Way too big for any one person to clean."

"That's gotta be a nightmare," she said. "I understand the compound is high-security conscious."

"Absolutely."

Flynn's phone rang just then. He pulled it from his pocket, looked at the number and sighed. "Levi never sleeps."

"SHE'S FINE. SHE has stitches in her bicep, and the arm's in a sling. Still looking a little pale and chalky, but she's got antibiotics and painkillers. We're at her place. A good night's sleep and she'll be that much better tomorrow," Flynn said. "Any update on what the police found?"

"Not yet. We will touch base in the morning. Just wanted to hear Anna was safe. Katina's beside herself here."

"Tell her Anna is fine."

"She's gone to bed. I'll knock and let her know. They can touch base in the morning too."

After that Levi hung up.

Flynn turned back to Anna. "Just like Flynn here, you have a family you aren't even aware of. And over time, it'll just get bigger and stronger," Logan said. He pulled his long length to an upright position. "If you guys think you're good for the night, I'll head home and crash."

Anna got up and ran over, throwing her good arm around him.

Gently he hugged her back, dropping a kiss on her forehead. "Now you be good. I don't want to see you back in the hospital anytime soon."

She beamed up at him. "I plan to never go back. Of course I might end up having to send Flynn so he knows what it feels like."

Flynn spoke from behind her. "As if."

She stepped back and said to Logan, "Thanks for looking after me so well."

They followed him to the front door and stood on the porch until he got into the truck and drove away.

Flynn closed the door, reset the alarm and said, "Come on. Let's get you upstairs to bed."

She looked around her. "What about this mess?"

"Tomorrow's another day. I can do the dishes in the morning. Right now, you're ready to crash, and I can't say I'm very far away from that myself."

He waited for her to climb the stairs, making sure all the lights were out downstairs, and then trailed up behind her. At her bedroom he stopped in the doorway. "You'll be okay for the night?"

She scrubbed her face with her left hand. "I'm just realizing how awkward this will be. I can't get my shirt off with my arm like this."

He saw the tears in the corners of her eyes and felt like a heel. "Come on. Let's get you ready for bed." He pulled back the bedding, took off her shoes and socks in seconds, and helped her out of her pants.

She looked at him and said, "You are very experienced at this."

That startled a laugh out of him. "Not as much as you may think. Now let's get that shirt off." He studied the sling first, then gently lifted her arms so he could pull it over her head. As if dealing with a baby, he carefully pulled one arm out of her T-shirt, then over her head and off her injured arm.

"What do you want to sleep in?"

She pointed at the dresser. "I have an oversize cotton T-shirt I like to use."

It was lying on top of the dresser. He grabbed it and came back to her. "Honey, the bra has to go."

She glanced down and winced. "Yeah, it so does." She stood, turned her back to him and said, "Unhook it please."

He did, and as she leaned forward, it managed to drop off her arms. Then she put her good one in the air, and he dropped the big T-shirt down over it and her head, followed slowly by her right arm. Gently he eased her sore arm back through the sling.

She turned around. "Damn that hurts."

"It'll feel much better in the morning."

She shook her head. "I doubt it." She kicked her dirty clothes off to the side and sat down on the edge of the bed. "I should brush my teeth, but I'm so damn tired."

"But you'll feel better. Come on. Let's get it done, then you can go to bed."

She let him lead her to the bathroom, where he put toothpaste on her toothbrush, ran it under the water and gave it to her. Then he grabbed the washcloth, doused it with warm water, and while she was brushing her teeth, he gently dabbed at the dried blood in her hair. His goal was to let her sleep without having this pull and tug through the night. He rinsed the cloth in more warm water and some soap, and when she was done with the toothbrush, he gently washed her face.

She smiled. "I feel like a two-year-old."

Using the same washcloth, he finished the job by washing her injured arm and both hands. "Sometimes we all need to be looked after. Now into bed with you."

She made her way back to the bed, crawled underneath the covers and lay down. She looked up at him expectantly.

She wasn't at all sure what she wanted, but he tucked the bedding up higher, bent down and kissed her on her forehead. Then he reached for the light.

"Wait."

He looked down at her. "What do you need?"

A flush stained her neck and cheeks a beautiful rose pink, but her eyes were direct and her voice clear when she answered, warm and lovingly, "You."

"Honey," he started to protest. He wanted her, but she was injured, so this was not a good idea.

She patted the side of the bed. "To sleep with me. Maybe just hold me until I fall asleep," she confessed. "It might hurt too much to do anything else. If you could see your way to sleeping beside me tonight ..."

He lowered his head and kissed her passionately, thoroughly, just enough for her to know he was there any time she was ready. "Absolutely. Just give me a minute to grab my stuff in the other room."

She nodded and shifted more comfortably, her eyes closing.

He went to the spare bedroom, where he had always stayed, then returned to hers. Exhausted, he prepped for bed. He'd planned on a shower, but there really wasn't a need tonight. He washed his face, brushed his teeth, and when he went back into the bedroom, found her almost asleep. He crawled in on his side. She turned to him instinctively, and he wrapped his arm gently around her, tucking her ever-so-slightly closer. But she moved in like a homing pigeon, nestling close to his chest.

"Thank you," she whispered.

He reached up and stroked her back gently. "My pleasure. There's nowhere I'd rather be right now."

With a happy smile she fell asleep.

He followed soon after.

Chapter 17

THE NEXT MORNING, Anna woke, surrounded by the intense heat pouring off Flynn. There was such a sense of well-being inside, she couldn't resist snuggling closer. She moved her injured arm experimentally. It didn't feel too bad.

She shifted away from the sleeping man beside her and made her way to the bathroom. She wondered if she should risk a shower. She could probably get the T-shirt off by herself. If she left the bandage on, would that be better or worse?

When she realized she still had dried blood in her hair, even though Flynn had done his best last night to wash it out, she decided the shower was mandatory. She glanced out the window to see bright, strong sunlight. So it was morning. And the animals were waiting.

She turned on the water, closed the door and waited for the water to warm up. She stripped off her panties and the T-shirt, taking great care not to bang up her arm as she did so, then stepped under the spray, bandage on. She'd do her best to keep it out of the water, but she knew that wasn't possible. Just standing under the heat as the warm water pounded down on her head felt soothing. With soap and a washcloth, she gave herself a good scrub, then did her best to shampoo her hair, washing it twice in order to get all the blood out. When she was done, she turned to find a shadow outside the glass doors.

A shriek escaped her, and she fell.

The door opened immediately. "Anna? It's just me."

She stared at him as the fear slowly drained. And then she got mad. "You could at least call out to let me know you're there," she cried.

He apologized. "I woke up and found you were gone. I came right away to see if you were in here. I just got here when you shrieked."

He held out a hand, which she used to get herself to her feet carefully because everything was so wet. That's when she realized she was standing fully nude in the shower in front of him. And he was standing fully nude out of the shower in front of her.

She shook her head. "Well, you might as well come in and get cleaned up."

He glanced at her in surprise, then grinned. "I wouldn't say no to that invitation."

"I was washing my hair," she said, "but I can't reach places on the right side."

"Here, I'll do that." He grabbed the shampoo and proceeded to wash her hair gently. He massaged every inch of her scalp until she was melting and moaning in pleasure.

"Oh, my God, where did you learn to do that? That's wonderful."

He moved her gently back under the stream and let the warm water rinse away all the suds. "Do you have any conditioner?"

She pointed at the bottle on the shelf. He grabbed it and put some in his hand. Rubbing his hands together, he gently stroked it through her hair.

She smiled. "Obviously you've practiced." And oddly

enough it didn't bother her a bit. He'd had a life before her, as she'd had one before him. As long as their future was built together on truth and love.

"I've never done this before in my life."

Her eyes flew open. "Really?"

He nodded and smiled down at her. He dropped a kiss on her nose. "Never. But I can see I might be interested in doing it often from now on."

This time, when he lowered his head, his hands still massaging her scalp, he took her lips in a deep passionate kiss, but he was so in control. Giving her time to say yes, giving her time to say no. Lady's choice, and she appreciated that. But what she wanted was him.

She'd never wanted any other man like she did him. Heat surrounded her inside, outside—his steam, the water's steam, the steam enveloping them in the small stall. More than that, her body was softening, dampening, opening, readying for him.

She slipped her good arm up around his neck and pressed against him from her slippery soapy hips to breasts. Skin to skin. Heat to heat. She kissed him back like she'd always wanted to. Need clawed at her.

This was the first chance they'd had to be together without all the horror. Not ideal as she was injured. But if they were careful …

He raised his head and pulled back slightly, in case she wanted to let him go. Instead, she wrapped her good arm tighter around him. He reached up to stroke her wet hair back off her face, his fingers caressing, gently loving. "Are you sure?" he whispered.

Anna looked up at him and smiled. "I've never been surer of anything in my life."

He looked around her at the shower and said, "Here or in the bed?"

She laughed. "Your choice. But personally I have no intention of walking anywhere." Her eyes lit with humor as she confessed, "I don't think I can."

He chuckled, shut off the water and said, "Maybe not, but for the sake of your arm, we're probably better getting you into bed, just so you don't hurt yourself more."

He grabbed a towel, wrapped it around her, then got a second one for himself. He gently helped her out and taking the towel, dried her off. As in every single inch of her. His strokes warm, lazy, and teasing.

She whispered, when she finally could find her voice, "I said I couldn't walk before. How the hell do you expect me to now?"

He gave himself a brisk rub over, tossed both towels to the floor and swept her up into his arms. "I never intended for you to walk anywhere."

He carried her to the bed and laid her down. Then he dropped beside her. She turned and wrapped her legs around him.

"Now that you've done so much to stoke the fire," she whispered, "how about you put it out?"

He would've chuckled, but she reached up and kissed him, hard. Her teeth biting the inside of his lip gently and then harder, kissing, licking, tasting her own passion, rising, driving her forward.

When he finally pulled his head back, his voice was hoarse. "Jesus."

She dragged his head back down. "Sorry, he's not available. In fact, nobody can help you now."

He gave a muffled laugh, followed by a strangled moan

and positioned himself between her thighs. She wrapped her legs around him tight, high up on his hips, and rubbed up and down against the hard shaft between them.

Flynn grabbed her hips, pulling her back, but she fought, climbing all over his frame. He gave a half laugh. "Sweetie, I haven't actually gotten where I need to be."

She gave him a half-lidded look. "Are you sure about that?" She pushed on his shoulders, and he rolled over. She went with him and sat up on her knees, straddling him. Whether by luck or design, she was poised right above his erection.

He stared up at her, and a wonderful smile crossed his face. "Oh, my God, you are the most beautiful thing I have ever seen."

She threw her head back and slowly lowered herself on his shaft. She was so wet, ready, and damn hot that he slid right inside. He grabbed her hips and thrust himself upward, seating himself fully and as deeply as he could go. She cried out, and with her hand on his shoulders to brace herself, she rode like the inner Valkyrie she was. She set a fast tempo, as nothing else would do, and drove them to the edge of the cliff. He reached down between them, his fingers sliding between her curls, finding the nub, and with a cry she threw her head back and exploded. He cupped her shoulders and slowly moved within.

With a shudder, she opened her eyes again and stared back down at him, one eyebrow raised.

He grinned and said, "Round two?"

She groaned. "Oh, my God. Why do I think this is going to be a long session?"

He laughed and gently stroked the nub in her curls, sending her blood pressure roaring to maximum once again.

This time it was a slower ride to the cliff but just as fantastic. She didn't want to go alone. She stretched down behind her and gently caught the soft globes between his legs and gave a squeeze.

It was his turn to groan. So she did it again, then slowly lifted herself up as if to remove herself from him. He grabbed her hips, forced her down. This time he lost control and drove harder, higher, deeper, and faster, and shouted when his climax ripped through him, his seed pulsing deep inside, sending her crashing to the shores below.

She collapsed on top of him and whispered, "I knew my arm wouldn't be a problem."

He gave a great big shudder and held her close. "If this is what you're like when you're injured," he whispered, "I can't imagine what you're like when you're not."

"For that, you'll have to wait a few days." She closed her eyes and nodded off.

FLYNN WAITED UNTIL she was asleep. He slowly and carefully disentangled himself from her arms and slid off the bed on his side, got to his feet and went to use the bathroom. He collected the towels, straightened them over the railing and dressed. He needed to check in with Levi this morning. It was late already, but she needed the sleep.

He'd take care of the animals and get some coffee going too. By the time she woke, she'd be ready for a cup.

With a happy whistle, he made his way downstairs and put on the coffee first. He grabbed his phone and called Levi while waiting. No answer.

Fine, he'd call back in a few minutes. He'd take care of the animals. He moved Jimbo and Duggy out to the big dog run. If Anna was feeling up to it, maybe they could take them both for a walk later. The dogs certainly needed it, but the dog run was big and gave them lots of space to jump around, which was exactly what they were doing.

He gave them fresh water, refilled their food dishes and let them eat in the pen. He checked on the cats, but they appeared to be snoozing, although two walked over for a greeting as he stepped inside. He spent a few minutes cuddling them, realizing just how much he enjoyed being able to pick up an animal and snuggle with it. The cats had lots of dry food. He'd mix in some canned, and they'd be good to go.

When he was done, he went back toward the house, still whistling. He grabbed his phone and tried Levi again. When the other end was answered, he asked, "Levi, any update?"

"Yes, but not one you're gonna like. He's been released."

Flynn couldn't believe what Levi was telling him. He heard the words, but the concept was just not computing. "What do you mean, he's out already?" He glanced at his watch. "It's only been, what, ten hours at the most?"

"His lawyers. He answered all the questions reasonably and gave alibis the police have checked. And apparently the detective in charge, some new upshot, spunky asshole, said he was allowed to leave the station but to stay in town."

"I don't give a shit what kind of lawyers he's got ..." Flynn strode up and down the kitchen, his fury rising. "You do realize he is on his way here then, right? It's either that, or he'll disappear, and we'll never see him again. Except we'll always be watching our backs."

"I know. I hear you. The DA's on it. Apparently they've sent men to pick him up again." Levi's voice was just as frustrated and angry as Flynn felt.

Flynn calmed down; his mind kicked in, working fast. "I haven't seen any sign of him. I was just out with the animals. I'm back inside now. I've got to get her up. We have to be ready. You know we can't trust him."

He strode toward the living room to look out the big window. No sign of Brendan. Good thing. "They could have kept him for twenty-four hours with no problem," Flynn snapped. "No way in hell should he have been let out."

Levi was still talking in his ear. "Keep me posted if you see him."

"I'll go check out the rest of the house now," Flynn said, turning. And he froze. "Levi …"

Brendan stood in front of him, a gun pointed at his chest. "Say hello and good-bye to Levi for me."

And he fired.

Chapter 18

ANNA WOKE WITH a jolt, the harsh cold sound still zinging through her memories into full wakefulness. Instantly, she knew she was alone in the room—and nude— lying on top of the covers.

Awkwardly, but ignoring the pain, she slipped on the panties and T-shirt she'd slept in before the shower and crept to the bedroom door. Downstairs she could hear a door bang, followed by running footsteps. She raced to her bedroom window to look out.

And saw Brendan running. He threw something into the neighbor's garbage and darted for a small black car. Within seconds, he drove down the street.

Panicked, she grabbed her phone and raced downstairs. She couldn't see anything in the kitchen or office. She barreled into the living room.

And fell to her knees screaming, "Flynn! Oh, my God. Flynn."

Blood poured from his chest. He'd been shot. She dialed 9-1-1 and slapped her hand over the wound, keeping pressure to slow the bleeding. "Help, please. He's been shot. Dear God. He's been shot in the chest."

"Calm down, we need to know your address. Are you still in danger?"

"My God. No, he ran away. He took off in a small black

car. It was Brendan. I saw him."

"Just stay on the line and stay calm. I have to dispatch somebody to your address. Is the front door unlocked?"

Anna twisted to find the door was open. "Yes. They should be able to see me from the front porch."

"Please stay on the line until we get you some help. Are you sure nobody else is there? Are you sure you're not in danger?"

"No, no, no. He ran away. Please hurry. Please, he can't die. Oh, my God. There's just so much blood."

"There is always a lot of blood with any injury. Don't let that affect you. Stay calm, stay collected and talk to him. If you can get any kind of response, let me know."

"No, he's totally unconscious. The color from his face, I mean... Oh, my God. It's just so white."

"And that's normal. Don't panic. Help is on the way."

"I need to phone other people."

"I need you to stay on the line. We have to keep this communication open."

She fretted but understood. In the distance she could hear the sirens. "Oh, thank God. I hear sirens."

"That's right. They should be there any minute now."

Before the woman stopped talking, she heard a screech of brakes outside, and two EMTs ran into the house. They took one look and moved her out of the way.

Into the phone she said, "I'm hanging up now. They're here."

She wrapped her arms tightly around her chest. She could hardly breathe. It was bad. It was so goddamn bad.

She called Levi. Blubbering into the phone, she said, "He shot him. Brendan shot Flynn." The tears choked her throat and stopped her voice from coming through. "The ambulance is here right now. But I don't think he'll live through this."

"I was on the phone with him when it happened. How bad is it? Do you remember exactly what happened?"

"I just woke up. I heard the shot, looked out the window, and I saw Brendan leaving. He threw the gun into the neighbor's garbage bin." She stared around the room. "I should go get it. I'm not even dressed."

"Stay calm. Somebody'll be there. We're going to find him. Hold tight. Do what you need to do to keep Flynn alive. Stay in touch. But don't run out there right now."

"You don't understand ... the gun. The gun that shot Flynn—I saw it. What if somebody grabs it? And I don't want to leave Flynn."

She stared down at her bare legs with his blood on them and his T-shirt in her hands. "There's just so much blood."

"We're in the vehicle already. Stay calm. We'll be there in a few minutes."

She gave a half laugh, one full of grief. "It's hardly minutes to get here."

"True, but Logan's on his way now too."

And she cried out, "Oh, my God. I should have called him first."

"It's not an issue. We called him. He's heading toward you right now."

Inside she wanted to feel relief. She wanted to know something would work out. But she knew it wouldn't. There was no way it could. "Levi, you have to see him. Oh, my God!"

And then she couldn't talk anymore for the tears clogging her throat. She sobbed quietly, deeply.

Levi's gentle voice whispered to her, "We've seen all of

us recover from some horrific injuries," he said. "I don't know how bad it is, but you have to hold on to faith. More than that, Flynn has to know you're there for him. He has to have something to fight for."

She nodded. It was the same with animals. She knew, when they gave up, it was all over. The spirit had to be there fighting, and it needed a reason. She wiped away her tears, taking several choking breaths and said, "I'm going upstairs to get dressed. I'll follow Flynn to the hospital. I don't want him to be alone right now."

In her bedroom, she dressed as quickly she could. She tossed the phone on the bed, not even knowing if she'd shut off the call. She quickly washed the blood off her hands and face, finished dressing, grabbed her phone and went back downstairs. She slipped on her shoes, grabbed her purse and headed outside. The EMTs were already loading Flynn into the back of the ambulance. She told the attendant, "Go. I'll follow."

She stood near her car, hugging her chest, watching as they took off. She didn't want him to go alone. But she also knew she would need wheels, and she would be damned if that Brendan asshole would get away with this. And for that she needed the gun.

She had a roll of poop bags in her pocket. She walked down to the garbage can where she'd seen Brendan throw the gun, opened the lid and looked inside. Sure enough it was here. She turned on the camera on her phone, took several pictures and then reached inside with the poop bag and grabbed it, carefully wrapping it inside.

As she turned around, Logan raced toward her. She started crying again. She held up the gun and said, "I saw him throw it in there. Oh, my God, I saw him throw it away."

Logan took her in his arms and held her close. "Did you actually see Brendan?"

She nodded. "From the back at first. Then he turned to look at the house as he threw the gun in the garbage." She motioned at the can where the gun had been. "And then he got into a small black car and took off. But it was too far away to get the license plate. I tried. I tried."

"Take it easy, sweetie. Take it easy. Let me take a quick look through the house and see if there's anything I need to do. Then we'll drive to the hospital."

Just then the cops came into the yard. Not one car, not two, but three. And she knew it wouldn't be easy to get out of her driveway now. Logan said in a low voice, "That's the same detective I spoke with earlier." The two men greeted each other. The gun was passed over.

Anna knew Logan was angry, but it was nothing compared to what she was feeling. She walked up to the cop and said, "The cops should never have let that asshole out. It's not enough that he shot me, but you had to wait until he actually killed somebody."

The cop didn't have anything to say. What could he anyway? It wasn't really his fault. It was the system's. He took the gun. "He's not dead yet. We'll do everything we can to ensure Brendan doesn't hurt anyone else. Can you show me the crime scene?"

Bitterly, she walked inside the front door of her house, following Logan. "Just put a bullet in his head. Save us all the trouble."

Inside she stopped and stared, tears flooding her eyes as she remembered the blood spurting out of Flynn. So much blood was in her living room. She knew that, whether Flynn survived or not, she was done with this house. She could not come into this living room ever again and not see the blood and the trauma she'd been through today. Nobody should have to. This place was going up for sale as soon as she could arrange it.

She turned to Logan. "I need to get to the hospital. Are you coming?"

"You're not driving."

She stared at him in determination. "I'm leaving now. With or without you."

He looked over at the cop and said, "You know what you have to do. You don't need us here."

The cop nodded. "Go. We'll catch you at the hospital."

She went with Logan to his truck, hopped inside and asked, "Should we tell Levi we're going?"

"Don't worry about it. I'll tell him."

She sat frozen, completely locked with fear as they drove to the hospital. It seemed like every mile they went, the fear grew worse. She just knew Flynn wouldn't make it.

"He'll make it. He's a fighter. You have to trust."

She stared at Logan blankly. "Trust what? They had him. They had Brendan, and they let him go."

"And they will get him again. This time they will throw away the key and forget he ever existed."

"It's too late for that. It's just way too late."

IT WAS CHAOS with lights, sirens, and screaming. Flynn lay caught in the dark cloud of confusion. But one thing he understood fully was the red fire that consumed his body from head to toe. So much pain. Everything hurt. Just to breathe hurt. He didn't dare move. He wasn't even sure he could. It seemed like so much weight was on his chest. Something was holding his legs and arms down. He struggled, trying to get to Anna. Danger was all around them. And he was fighting. He had to save her. He couldn't let her get hurt again. Not anymore.

And yet, he could do nothing. He struggled and struggled, but he knew nothing came of it. He wanted his arms and legs to move, but he couldn't get them to. As he fought against the heavy pain, with huge blackened hands reaching out for him, he knew he didn't want to go in that direction. He tried to get away from them. But they moved inexorably toward him.

He wanted to run. He wanted to cry out. In his mind was this endless long-drawn-out scream of "*Noooo.*" But nothing stopped the march of those hands. They latched on to his heart, mind, and soul. They dragged him back under into the murky depths of unconsciousness.

But he knew what they were. He knew they were really the fingers of death.

Chapter 19

THERE WAS NOTHING to do but wait. There was no update. There was no doctor coming in to give her a status. Flynn was in emergency surgery. Nobody knew anything.

Levi and Ice had arrived. Stone and Merk had gone to her house. Logan was at the hospital with her. Rhodes had gone down to the police headquarters. Apparently, he knew several cops and would raise Cain.

There wasn't enough Cain in this world for anybody to raise to make her happy. She had one goal now: to ensure Flynn survived. And if she had a secondary, it was: make certain Brendan didn't. But she had no idea how to get her hands on him.

Levi sat down next to her; Ice on the other side with her arm around Anna's shoulders. She said, "We need to hear your words. Exactly what you saw."

She stared at them, more tears burning her eyes, so hot with fear that nothing would cool them, and she once again explained what she'd seen. "I think it was the shot that woke me up." She shook her head. "After that it's all a blur. Just a painful, agonizing blur."

"At least it did wake you up. Flynn got attention as fast as possible. You have to hold on to that. Plus, you can confirm it was Brendan, and you found the weapon."

"I guess it proves Brendan was after Flynn all along. He could have come upstairs and shot me. I don't know that I would've been awake and aware enough to have avoided it."

Ice gripped her fingers. "Thank God he didn't."

Anna turned to look at Ice. "Did you guys find his car? Did the cops get the gun?"

"Yes and yes. You gave the gun to Logan, and he gave it to the cops."

Anna frowned. "Right. I remember that." She waved a hand. "Honestly, everything's a blur. I don't really understand the sequence of what happened."

"And you don't need to. The police are running the ballistics on the gun. We think the black car you saw at your house might've been Brendan's brother's."

At that Anna gave a half snort. "The brother who doesn't believe Brendan would do anything, right?"

"Well, he might be changing his mind now," Levi said coolly. "He's down at the police station. Rhodes is clueing him in."

"Good. He should be locked up too." Anna glared at Levi. "I suppose it's his damn lawyer connections that got his brother out in the first place."

"It's possible." Levi shrugged. "There's just no reason sometimes."

"Right now I know the reason. The best murderer is a dead one. I'm now a believer in the death sentence." She slumped back in the chair and leaned her head back.

Ice looked at her. "Did you have your arm checked out?"

Her head rolled over toward Ice, and she asked, "What's wrong with my arm?"

She could hear the heavy sigh from Ice and remembered her stitches from the bullet wound last night. She glanced down to see fresh blood all over the bandaged injury. She stared at it in surprise. "No idea how that happened. I can't feel it, so it can't be bad."

"You can't feel it because you're in shock. But those are stitches, and if you've ripped them, we need to get them looked at."

"I'm not leaving," she said firmly.

But Ice wasn't having anything to do with that. "There's stupidity, and then there is stupidity. We only deal with one kind. Right now Flynn's being taken care of. Now you need to be as well." And with a firm grip on her uninjured arm, Ice forced Anna to her feet and said, "Come with me now."

Ice, just like all the men in the company, was a force not to be ignored. Anna turned to look back at Levi as Ice dragged her toward the doorway.

"Don't let him be alone," Anna cried out.

"He'll be in surgery for several more hours. You'll be back before he comes out. If I hear anything, I'll let you know. And I promise, I won't leave him alone."

Sobbing quietly, Anna let Ice drag her down to the emergency area. It was full but not crazy. Ice walked over to one of the nurses and explained what happened. As it was, it was the same nurse she'd had the previous evening.

She took one look at Anna and asked, "Oh, my dear, you've had a terrible twenty-four hours, haven't you?"

Anna, hating to be the watering pot, turned and scrubbed her face. "It's probably nothing. Ice is just worrying over the blood."

"And she's right to." The nurse led Anna to a bed and made her sit down. She left a moment and came back with scissors, quickly cutting off the bandage. "It's not too bad though." She patted Anna on her good arm and said, "I'll let the doctor know in case he wants to see you too."

As her eyes went down to study the wound, Anna realized she probably needed to get it taken care of, but she hated to think about herself when Flynn had suffered so much.

"You have to consider your own health," Ice said. "The animals will need you, as will Flynn as soon as he wakes up."

Anna stared at her. "I didn't think about that."

And she hadn't. She'd been so locked into the immediate negativity, she hadn't seen that, if he did survive the surgery, somebody must take care of him. And she did have animals to look after. Therefore, she needed her dominant arm, which was the one that was injured.

She looked down at the blood. "You are right. I should've gotten it looked at. But I really didn't notice."

"Of course not," Ice said in a gentle voice. "But once you take care of the first emergency, it's very important to take a look around and see what needs to be dealt with next."

"That's your military training," Anna said. "Most people don't think like that."

"It's not just that training or even my medical training. But it is from a life lived on the edge all the time. Which we still are." Ice smiled at Anna. "You got the right stuff. Your instincts are strong and sound. But you have to learn to look after yourself. Because without that, it's almost impossible to do the same for those around us. And regardless of what happens, we're still females. We tend to be nurturers. So Flynn will need your help. If you aren't strong enough to help him, he won't get the care he deserves."

Anna nodded. She grabbed a tissue from the Kleenex box, wiped her eyes and blew her nose awkwardly with her left hand. She wasn't very good at looking after herself that way. She'd have to change that. Eventually.

Ice's phone rang. And the nurse returned. With her attention caught between what the nurse was doing and the phone conversation Ice was having with Rhodes at the police station, Anna couldn't keep track. By the time the nurse was done rebandaging her arm, it was on fire.

The nurse turned to her and asked, "Did you manage to bring any of your painkillers with you when you came to the hospital?"

"No. They're back at the house. And I probably won't be allowed in for a while. It's full of cops right now."

The nurse disappeared and returned a few minutes later with a small bottle. "There are enough here to get you through the day. Somebody should be allowed back into the house to at least get your medications."

She accepted them gratefully. "Thank you. I'm sure somebody will be able to." She managed to hop off the bed but hung on for a moment as the room swayed around her.

Ice looked at her sharply. "Have you eaten?"

She stared at Ice blankly. Then shook her head. "No, I haven't."

Ice nodded as if that was exactly what she figured. "Let me phone Levi to confirm there is no change, then I'm taking you to the cafeteria."

They waited in the hallway for Levi to confirm Flynn was still in surgery. At the cafeteria, they filled two trays and went to a table at the back of the room where they sat down and ate. Anna didn't want any juice, but Ice insisted. "I can't have you passing out."

Every time Ice opened her mouth, it was logical, reasonable, and made so much sense that Anna found herself following Ice's instructions without question. She poured the orange juice into a glass and drank half of it down. It didn't take long for her to start feeling better. As she looked at her omelet, she realized she really was hungry. It was just so hard to eat, knowing Flynn was upstairs.

Ice reached across the table and grabbed her hand. "Remember, you're eating for you, so you can be strong enough to look after him."

With a ghost of a smile, she teased Ice. "You get away with that line a lot."

Ice smiled. "I've been where you are."

She studied Ice, seeing the remembered pain and agony of almost losing somebody. Anna nodded. "I believe you." And she tackled her omelet. She made it almost all the way through before she slowed down. She stared at the last couple bites and shook her head. "I don't think I can do it."

"Finish your eggs—leave the toast."

Anna stuffed down the last of the omelet and pushed back her tray. A large hand reached over her shoulder, grabbing the toast off her plate, as the unmistakable Stone sat down beside them. She studied him. "You have any news?"

"I just came from your house. The cops are all over the place. It looks like Brendan walked in the front door and surprised Flynn or waited until he showed up. What I'm thinking is that Flynn put on coffee and went to look after the animals. When he came back in, Brendan was waiting for him." She could see it happen just like that in her head. It didn't make it any easier. "Why is it nobody has picked up Brendan?" She caught Ice and Stone exchanging glances. "What?"

"First, we have to find him. And second, he won't be picked up. He's likely to end up in a shootout to avoid capture."

"Good," she said in a hard voice. "As much as I like the idea of that man wasting away in a prison somewhere, I don't want to take the chance of him coming back out anytime in the future and ruining my life again. I want him dead. He deserves nothing less."

Stone grinned, studying her. "She's bloodthirsty. I like that." And he took a big bite out of her toast.

Just then both Ice and Stone's phones went off. They looked at the number. Ice said, "That's Levi. Surgery is over."

But they were talking to the air. She'd already bolted to her feet and raced back to Flynn.

MORE VOICES. MORE voices. And yet, more voices. Screaming, yelling, then quiet conversation. Between some kind of a mechanical scream in a weird tone, he couldn't quite make out what was being said. But once the machinery stopped, he heard the doctor say, "He's back."

Flynn wondered who'd gone and come back, and why anybody gave a shit. It was so hard to sort out the noises. But at least the pain was better. His chest didn't feel like it was closing in on him. He still couldn't move—a sense of being paralyzed. And he couldn't think of anything worse. It wasn't how he wanted to live his life. He tried to yell, "Help!"

But nobody answered.

"Hello."

He could hear the word in his mind, but he knew his lips weren't moving. He didn't think they could. He tried to open his eyes, turn his head. Nothing worked. The struggle was too much. The cotton batting around him closed in on him. But at least those long fingers of death weren't dragging him under. He wanted to roll over onto his side, but again he couldn't. He gave up the effort and let himself succumb to the clouds, willing them to carry him away.

Chapter 20

ANNA BURST INTO the waiting room to see Levi and the doctor's heads bent together. They both looked up at her as she made a mad dash into the room. Levi reached out to slow her pace. "He's alive. Take it easy. He's alive."

All the color washed out of her face as relief made her sway on her feet. She stared at the doctor, searching, looking for reassurance. "Will he be okay?"

"He's not out of hot water yet. He has a long road to recovery, but his prognosis is a whole lot better than it was. The bullet went into the chest cavity, nicked the heart at the top and went through, lodging into a rib in his back. We got the bullet out, and he's been stitched up. He's lost a lot of blood, and we had to give him several units." He sighed. "We lost him on the table."

"Lost him?" At that she gripped Levi's hands.

"His heart stopped while we were working on him. But we brought him back. He'll be just fine."

"Hold on to that thought," Levi told her.

She glanced toward the door. "When can I see him?"

The doctor shook his head. "Not until I get him settled in ICU. The next twenty-four hours are critical."

She nodded, biting her lower lip. Tears once again formed in her eyes. "Thank you so much for saving him."

He reached out and patted her shoulder. "He's a fighter.

Everybody deserves a chance to live, but when they fight, it makes our job so much easier." With a quiet smile he turned and walked off.

Anna walked to the bench against the wall and collapsed. "Oh, thank God," she whispered.

She didn't know what to do. All she could think about was that he'd survived the surgery and his chances were good. "We have to catch Brendan. Make sure he can never try this again."

"We will," Levi said. "Brendan's luck has run out."

She turned to study him. "Unless you know something I don't, I don't see how you can be so sure. That guy has been getting away with murder. Literally." She turned to study the double doors marked Surgery where Flynn still was. "Any way we can set a trap for him? Do you think he would go after Flynn again?"

Levi looked at her. "He might. He's gone through a lot of trouble already. What are you thinking?"

"Tell his brother how Brendan missed his mark, that Flynn will be home soon. There was some metal in his pocket, and the bullet was deflected. Brendan wasn't there long enough to see the blood that was everywhere. So he can't possibly know how good a shot he actually made. And then set up at my house and wait for him."

"You're assuming his brother will tell him."

"I'm assuming his brother has already gone overboard trying to protect him, and at some point the two will talk over the next few days." She shrugged. "Maybe even to just reassure Brendan he's not up for murder charges."

The others in the room looked at each other.

"That might work. But that's leaving a lot open to chance."

"Chance is all we have. He's made several attempts at my house. If he thought he'd missed, this time he might be so frustrated and enraged he would come back for one final move to kill Flynn for sure."

"She's right," Stone said. "Brendan's always been a bit of a wild card. But I'm not sure about his brother. He's a good guy. If he understands how out-of-control Brendan is right now, and the fact that he just shot Flynn in cold blood, I don't think he would protect him. I think he would help us catch Brendan before he hurts anybody else."

Just then the double doors opened, and Flynn was wheeled out. Anna dashed to his side, her hand over her mouth. He was unconscious, pure white, covered in tubes and blankets.

She turned to the others and said, "Set it up. I'll play my part. I don't want this to happen to anybody else ever again. I'm going in ICU with Flynn."

The nurse shook her head and said, "Only family can be in ICU."

Anna said, "I'm the only family he's got." She shot a hard glance at the three other medical personnel in scrubs, daring them to argue. Not one of them did. They smiled and gave her a nod.

In a low voice Ice called out, "Welcome to the family."

Anna grinned. It felt good to belong.

Following the nurses and orderly, she waited until Flynn was moved into recovery. Then she grabbed the visitor's chair and settled in for a long wait. She wasn't leaving his side. Not again.

FLYNN OPENED HIS eyes and slammed them shut again. The

light was so bright it hurt. He lay motionless for several long moments, then tried again. He opened them just enough so he could see he was in a room. Likely a hospital room from all the white around him.

Rolling his head to the side, he saw the IV line and machinery all around. Sure enough he was in a hospital bed. He remembered vaguely what happened. But it was disjointed and jumbled in his head. Until the name *Brendan* whispered through his mind. With a flash he was back in the living room, staring at Brendan as he raised a gun and fired. Flynn remembered the crushing pain as his body fell to the floor.

That answered how he got here. Moving carefully, he rolled his head to the other side and smiled. Curled up in the corner of the visitor's chair, feet tucked under her, her head resting on the back of the chair, was a sleeping Anna.

No wonder he'd survived. He had had his own guardian angel watching over him. He studied her pale skin and the bags under her eyes, realizing she'd probably been here since he'd been shot. She'd been sleeping upstairs at the time. He was just damn glad Brendan hadn't gone up and shot her too. He saw a fresh bandage on her arm. He hadn't been out so long that her arm had healed. That was good. A couple days he could deal with. He just didn't want to be coming out from weeks in a coma. Apparently that played havoc with the muscles.

Suddenly, as if realizing he was staring at her, her eyes flew open. She gazed at him for a long moment in disbelief, then bounded to her feet.

"Oh, my God. You're awake."

He smiled. "I am."

She reached down and gently picked up his hand. She brought it to her lips and kissed it. "I was so worried."

"I remember Brendan shooting me," he admitted. "What happened after that, I have no idea."

"I'll fill you in." And she did briefly. It was enough for him to get an idea.

"How long have I been out?"

"Your surgery was yesterday morning. You've surfaced and gone under a couple times but not really conscious."

"I suppose you've been sitting here, waiting all this time?"

She smiled. In a teasing voice she asked, "Are you telling me, if it was me in this hospital bed, you wouldn't be standing where I am?"

He squeezed her hand. "You know I would."

She glanced around and winced. "I did have to lie."

"Lie?"

"Yes. Only family is allowed in ICU."

And then he understood. His heart warmed, and his smile turned teasing. "Well, in truth that was just jumping the gun a little bit."

She sat down at the side of the bed and eyed him carefully. He stretched up a long finger and placed it across her lips. Immediately she kissed it. "You will be part of the family," he told her. "No way am I letting my guardian angel slip through my fingers." He watched the moisture well up in her eyes.

The door opened, letting in a nurse who scolded Anna. "You were supposed to let us know immediately when he woke up."

Anna jumped back and dropped his hand. "I'm so sorry. He just woke up though."

The nurse bustled around, brushing Anna out of the way. Flynn lay quietly as she ran him through a series of tests and questions. She then turned to Anna and said, "The doctor's on the way. When he comes, you'll need to step out."

Flynn watched as Anna collected her sweater, purse, several notepads, and a laptop. It looked like she'd planned to be here for a while. Just as she was about to exit, he called, "I love you, Anna."

She turned and gave him a special smile that made his heart warm.

The nurse stepped in between the two of them, and he never got to hear or see her reaction. Then the door was closed. It opened almost immediately as the doctor stepped in.

And his focus turned to the other people who'd saved his life.

Chapter 21

WHEN ANNA WAS finally allowed back into Flynn's room, he was ready to nod off again. They'd given him a sedative after changing the tubes and cleaning his wound. And he was in a great deal of pain, the nurse explained. While Anna had been outside waiting, she'd informed everybody Flynn was awake.

She sat back down in the visitor's chair, and Levi texted her.

Neil, Brendan's brother, has agreed to help. The word has already gone out to Brendan that Flynn wasn't badly hurt and is going home this afternoon.

She texted back:

Good. Do you want me to go home?
No. We'll handle this.

Perfect. She didn't want to leave Flynn, but if she must to keep him safe, then that was what she'd do.

Just make sure it works. I want to know that asshole can't get at us again.

Keep us updated on Flynn's condition. We'll let you know how it goes.

She put down her phone, curled up in the chair and closed her eyes. Now that Flynn had woken up, recognized her, and seemed to be improving, she could finally relax. Especially with Levi setting up a plan to take out Brendan. She wouldn't really be able to truly rest until he was, but everybody was doing their part, and she really appreciated that. She hadn't gotten any sleep last night, just drifted in and out. Every time she heard a sound, she woke up, thinking Flynn needed something. But now she yawned deeply, used her hand to cushion her cheek a little and drifted off to sleep.

She woke up a little bit later, seeing one of the doctors walking back into the room. She could expect a lot of that now. They would assess when to move him from ICU over to the main hospital. She hoped it wasn't too fast. She knew how quickly his condition could downgrade. She didn't want that for Flynn.

She closed her eyes again and then it hit her. She opened her eyes slowly to see the doctor walking to the IV line. He had a needle in his hand, about to inject something into Flynn's IV bag.

"What are you doing?"

The man turned to her, and she recognized him. Brendan.

"You." She bolted off the chair, racing toward him with her nails ready to scratch the hell out of him. She had no weapon, and he was a pro, but no way in hell was he getting close to Flynn.

She threw herself at him, sending him off balance, but still on his feet, knocking the needle from his hand. It skittered across the floor, and she was on him like a leech. He tried to drag her off, but she clung to him, dug her nails in his back and bit him hard in the neck, her teeth connecting with the soft tissue and going as deep as she could dig them in.

He roared in pain. She could feel his blood gush into her mouth, but she hung on. He tripped and fell to his knees, but she wouldn't let go. Suddenly she was wrenched off and flung clear. And then he was on top of her, both on the floor now.

"You stupid bitch."

He hit her hard in the face.

Pain slammed into her. She knew she'd lost the one chance of attack she had available to her. She reached for anything that could be used as a weapon. And her hand closed over the needle he'd dropped.

He struggled to his knees, his hand over the wound on his neck.

She sat up and stabbed him in the neck with the needle and plunged deep, shoving its contents into his body.

"No," he cried out. "You can't do that. He has to pay for what he did to me. He got me kicked out. Ruined my life."

"No," she yelled. "It wasn't him."

She hopped to her feet and backed away, spitting out his blood then wiping her mouth clean. "You did that all on your own." And she saw the truth slowly dawn even as his eyes started to glaze over.

She turned, opening the door between her and the nurses' station, screaming, "Help, please, help. He tried to murder the patient."

Several people ran toward her. With relief she saw one of them was a security guard. She turned to glance back at Brendan, but he was flat on the floor, his body jerking spasmodically.

"What happened to him?" the nurse asked.

Anna pointed at the needle in his neck. "He tried to inject that into Flynn's IV line. But I shoved it into him instead."

"You know for sure he was trying to kill him?" a different nurse asked.

Anna turned to face the security guard now on the scene. "He's the one who shot Flynn in the first place. He also shot me." She motioned at her arm. "I know for sure he killed another man too."

The security guard checked on Brendan, his weapon out and ready. But just as suddenly, Brendan stopped jerking. One of the nurses approached carefully, bent down and checked for a pulse. She looked up at Anna and said, "He's dead."

From the bed came a weak voice. "Good. And I concur with what Anna said. That's Brendan McAllister. He's the one who shot me."

The nurse straightened and said, "Well, he won't be shooting anybody else ever again."

Anna raced to Flynn's bedside and gently flung herself over him. She sobbed uncontrollably now.

Flynn wrapped an arm around her and held her close. "Easy, baby. Easy. You did good." He glanced at the other people in the room, then forgot all about them as he focused solely on Anna.

She sobbed even more. "Oh, my God. I couldn't believe it was him. Levi and the others are setting a trap right now at my house."

Flynn smiled. He reached up and wiped away the tears from her eyes. "That was always Brendan. Never doing the expected."

She stared at Flynn, then sat down heavily. "I killed him. Dear God. I killed a man."

Flynn nodded. "I'm so sorry you had to do that, honey."

She stared at him for a moment and then said defiantly, "I'm not. He was trying to kill you. For that, I would kill him all over again."

He gently stroked her lips and whispered, "So feisty. I like that."

She smiled down at him. "I love you. I never got a chance to say that before."

His hand slipped behind her neck, and he tugged her downward. When her lips were just above his, he whispered, "And I love you too."

She kissed him. Not hard, but with a sweetness that defined the moment in a way she had never expected.

When she lifted her head again, he said, "I believe I mentioned a position that might be of interest to you earlier."

She frowned, her eyebrows coming together as she studied his face to see a tiny smile playing at the corner of his mouth. "What position was that?" she whispered.

He tugged her gently forward until her head was just above his again. "The position of my wife."

She gasped in joy. "Do you mean it?"

He smiled. "Remember that part about not letting my guardian angel go?"

"You want to marry me because I saved your life, right?" she asked cautiously. "You'd be taking on the animals, the shelter, and me."

He chuckled. "Honey, I have a lot of reasons why I want to marry you. That just happens to be icing on top. I want to marry you because I want to wake up to you every morning.

I want to see you first thing when I open my eyes and know my days will turn out perfectly because you're there with me."

She sniffled back more tears. "That's a beautiful thing to say."

"And yet, you have not answered." His eyes lost some of the teasing.

"The answer is yes," she said softly. "There was never any doubt in my mind you were the one for me. I just didn't have an excuse to come back and see you again. But I was desperate to find one."

"Not to worry. I would've been there that same day if you hadn't come racing into the compound instead."

They smiled at each other in joy.

"Ice already welcomed me to the family," he said quietly, then chuckled. "She's very astute."

"She welcomed me to the family, here in the hospital," Anna said. "She's also a little scary."

"Agreed. But she's all heart."

"And you're mine. Truly you're my hero. And the hero for my animals." Anna smirked. "I think that makes you my Hero for the Homeless."

"Better not let Levi hear that," he warned. "Although Ice will love it."

With a misty smile, she whispered, "I didn't think I'd survive when I realized how badly hurt you were."

"I'm tough," he said. "Besides, I had the best thing in the world to live for."

When she raised an eyebrow in silent question, he pulled her head down once again for his kiss, and just before he claimed her lips, he whispered, "You."

Epilogue

L OGAN WALKED DOWN the hospital corridor. He couldn't believe the way the events had gone down. He was damn grateful but, at the same time, thought, *how typical of Brendan*. Logan shifted the roses in his arm. They were more for Anna than Flynn.

As he walked in, he saw lots of other flowers around the room. He laughed. "I guess you didn't need these." He handed them to Anna.

She accepted them, threw her arms around his neck and gave him a big hug.

He kissed her on her cheek. "Glad to see our warrior woman doing so well."

She laughed a little and put a smile on her face. "I don't know about the warrior-woman thing," she said, "but I'm doing just fine. Especially now that Flynn's doing okay."

Logan turned toward Flynn. "Not too bad, buddy. Get yourself shot and engaged at the same time."

Flynn gave him a lazy glance. "Recovery is a bitch," he said easily. "But I'm blessed with my own guardian angel." He reached out a hand, and Anna was there to grab hold of it.

Logan laughed. "I can see that. Too bad she doesn't have a sister. Maybe she could share some of that loving, healing light."

"You'll find your own light one day," Anna promised.

He looked at her, cocked his head to the side and said, "I'm not so sure about that."

She gave him a special smile and said, "I am."

He shook his head. "Maybe. But I doubt it."

Still, as he looked at how happy his friend was, he realized they truly were blessed. His time would come. But maybe not for a long while yet. Maybe. He was okay with that.

Hopefully.

This concludes Book 5 of Heroes for Hire: Flynn's Firecracker.

Read about Logan's Light: Heroes for Hire, Book 6

Heroes for Hire: Logan's Light (Book #6)

Logan heads to Boston on an intelligence reconnaissance mission for Legendary Securities. His investigation plunges him—and the inadvertent partner he picks up along the way—into the dark, chilling world of human trafficking.

The last thing Alina remembers was having coffee at the hospital cafe where she's employed. Awakening in a strange apartment, she finds herself tied up. Until Logan appeared, seemingly out of nowhere, and rescued her, she'd feared life as she'd known it was over.

The traffickers have a quota and letting even one potential moneymaker go isn't in the cards. Alina is far from the only victim. On the run together, Logan and Alina race against time, no longer certain who's the hunted and who's the prey in the sordid, heartbreaking underworld they've descended into.

Book 6 is available now!

To find out more visit Dale Mayer's website.

https://geni.us/DMLoganUniversal

Other Military Series by Dale Mayer

SEALs of Honor

Heroes for Hire

SEALs of Steel

The K9 Files

The Mavericks

Bullards Battle

Hathaway House

Terkel's Team

Ryland's Reach: Bullard's Battle (Book #1)

Welcome to a new stand-alone but interconnected series from Dale Mayer. This is Bullard's story—and that of his team's. All raw, rough, incredibly capable men who have one goal: to find out who was behind the attack on their leader, before the attacker, or attackers, return to finish the job.

Stay tuned for more nonstop action as the men narrow down their suspects … and find a way to let love back into their own empty lives.

His rescue from the ocean after a horrible plane explosion was his top priority, in any way, shape, or form. A small sailboat and a nurse to do the job was more than Ryland hoped for.

When Tabi somehow drags him and his buddy Garret onboard and surprisingly gets them to a naval ship close by, Ryland figures he'd used up all his luck and his friend's too. Sure enough, those who attacked the plane they were in weren't content to let him slowly die in the ocean. No. Surviving had made him a target all over again.

Tabi isn't expecting her sailing holiday to include the rescue of two badly injured men and then to end with the loss of her beloved sailboat. Her instincts save them, but now she finds it tough to let them go—even as more of Bullard's team members come to them—until it becomes apparent that not only are Bullard and his men still targets ... but she is too.

B ULLARD CHECKED THAT the helicopter was loaded with their bags and that his men were ready to leave.

He walked back one more time, his gaze on Ice. She'd never looked happier, never looked more perfect. His heart ached, but he knew she remained a caring friend and always would be. He opened his arms; she ran into them, and he held her close, whispering, "The offer still stands."

She leaned back and smiled up at him. "Maybe if and when Levi's been gone for a long enough time for me to forget," she said in all seriousness.

"That's not happening. You two, now three, will live long and happy lives together," he said, smiling down at the woman knew to be the most beautiful, inside and out. She would never be his, but he always kept a little corner of his heart open and available, in case she wanted to surprise him and to slide inside.

And then he realized she'd already been a part of his heart all this time. That was a good ten to fifteen years by now. But she kept herself in the friend category, and he understood because she and Levi, partners and now parents, were perfect together.

Bullard reached out and shook Levi's hand. "It was a hell of a blast," he said. "When you guys do a big splash, you really do a *big* splash."

Ice laughed. "A few days at home sounds perfect for me now."

"It looks great," he said, his hands on his hips as he surveyed the people in the massive pool surrounded by the palm trees, all designed and decked out by Ice. Right beside all the war machines that he heartily approved of. He grinned at her. "When are you coming over to visit?" His gaze went to Levi, raising his eyebrows back at her. "You guys should come over for a week or two or three."

"It's not a bad idea," Levi said. "We could use a long holiday, just not yet."

"That sounds familiar." Bullard grinned. "Anyway, I'm off. We'll hit the airport and then pick up the plane and head home." He added, "As always, call if you need me."

Everybody raised a hand as he returned to the helicopter and his buddy who was flying him to the airport. Ice had volunteered to shuttle him there, but he hadn't wanted to take her away from her family or to prolong the goodbye. He hopped inside, waving at everybody as the helicopter lifted. Two of his men, Ryland and Garret, were in the back seats. They always traveled with him.

Bullard would pick up the rest of his men in Australia. He stared down at the compound as he flew overhead. He preferred his compound at home, but damn they'd done a nice job here.

With everybody on the ground screaming goodbye, Bullard sailed over Houston, heading toward the airport. His two men never said a word. They all knew how he felt about Ice. But not one of them would cross that line and say anything. At least not if they expected to still have jobs.

It was one thing to fall in love with another man's woman, but another thing to fall in love with a woman who was so unique, so different, and so absolutely perfect that you knew, just knew, there was no hope of finding anybody else like her. But she and Levi had been together way before Bullard had ever met her, which made it that much more heartbreaking.

Still, he'd turned and looked forward. He had a full roster of jobs himself to focus on when he got home. Part of him was tired of the life; another part of him couldn't wait to head out on the next adventure. He managed to run everything from his command centers in one or two of his locations. He'd spent a lot of time and effort at the second one and kept a full team at both locations, yet preferred to spend most of his time at the old one. It felt more like home to him, and he'd like to be there now, but still had many more days before that could happen.

The helicopter lowered to the tarmac, he stepped out, said his goodbyes and walked across to where his private plane waited. It was one of the things that he loved, being a pilot of both helicopters and airplanes, and owning both birds himself.

That again was another way he and Ice were part of the same team, of the same mind-set. He'd been looking for another woman like Ice for himself, but no such luck. Sure, lots were around for short-term relationships, but most of them couldn't handle his lifestyle or the violence of the world that he lived in. He understood that.

The ones who did had a hard edge to them that he found difficult to live with. Bullard appreciated everybody's being alert and aware, but if there wasn't some softness in the women, they seemed to turn cold all the way through.

As he boarded his small plane, Ryland and Garret following behind, Bullard called out in his loud voice, "Let's go, slow pokes. We've got a long flight ahead of us."

The men grinned, confident Bullard was teasing, as was his usual routine during their off-hours.

"Well, we're ready, not sure about you though ..." Ryland said, smirking.

"We're waiting on you this time," Garret added with a chuckle. "Good thing you're the boss."

Bullard grinned at his two right-hand men. "Isn't that the truth?" He dropped his bags at one of the guys' feet and said, "Stow all this stuff, will you? I want to get our flight path cleared and get the hell out of here."

They'd all enjoyed the break. He tried to get over once a year to visit Ice and Levi and same in reverse. But it was time to get back to business. He started up the engines, got confirmation from the tower. They were heading to Australia for this next job. He really wanted to go straight back to Africa, but it would be a while yet. They'd refuel in Honolulu.

Ryland came in and sat down in the copilot's spot, buckled in, then asked, "You ready?"

Bullard laughed. "When have you ever known me *not* to be ready?" At that, he taxied down the runway. Before long he was up in the air, at cruising level, and heading to Hawaii. "Gotta love these views from up here," Bullard said. "This place is magical."

"It is once you get up above all the smog," he said. "Why Australia again?"

"Remember how we were supposed to check out that newest compound in Australia that I've had my eye on? Besides the alpha team is coming off that ugly job in Sydney. We'll give them a day or two of R&R then head home."

"Right. We could have some equally ugly payback on that job."

Bullard shrugged. "That goes for most of our jobs. It's the life."

"And don't you have enough compounds to look after?"

"Yes I do, but that kid in me still looks to take over the world. Just remember that."

"Better you go home to Africa and look after your first two compounds," Ryland said.

"Maybe," Bullard admitted. "But it seems hard to not continue expanding."

"You need a partner," Ryland said abruptly. "That might ease the savage beast inside. Keep you home more."

"Well, the only one I like," he said, "is married to my best friend."

"I'm sorry about that," Ryland said quietly. "What a shit deal."

"No," Bullard said. "I came on the scene last. They were always meant to be together. Especially now they are a family."

"If you say so," Ryland said.

Bullard nodded. "Damn right, I say so."

And that set the tone for the next many hours. They landed in Hawaii, and while they fueled up everybody got off to stretch their legs by walking around outside a bit as this was a small private airstrip, not exactly full of hangars and tourists. Then they hopped back on board again for takeoff.

"I can fly," Ryland offered as they took off.

"We'll switch in a bit," Bullard said. "Surprisingly, I'm doing okay yet, but I'll let you take her down."

"Yeah, it's still a long flight," Ryland said studying the islands below. It was a stunning view of the area.

"I love the islands here. Sometimes I just wonder about the benefit of, you know, crashing into the sea, coming up on a deserted island, and finding the simple life again," Bullard said with a laugh.

"I hear you," Ryland said. "Every once in a while, I wonder the same."

Several hours later Ryland looked up and said abruptly, "We've made good time considering we've already passed Fiji."

Bullard yawned.

"Let's switch."

Bullard smiled, nodded, and said, "Fine. I'll hand it over to you."

Just then a funny noise came from the engine on the right side.

They looked at each other, and Ryland said, "Uh-oh. That's not good news."

Boom!

And the plane exploded.

Find Bullard's Battle (Book #1) here!

To find out more visit Dale Mayer's website.

https://geni.us/DMRylandUniversal

Damon's Deal: Terkel's Team (Book #1)

Welcome to a brand-new connected series of intrigue, betrayal, and ... murder, from the *USA Today* best-selling author Dale Mayer. A series with all the elements you've come to love, plus so much more... including psychics!

A betrayal from within has Terkel frantic to protect those he can, as his team falls one by one, from a murderous killer he helped create.

ICE POURED HERSELF a coffee and sat down at the compound's massive dining room table with the others. When her phone rang, she smiled at the number displayed. "Hey, Terk. How're you doing?" She put the call on Speakerphone.

"I'm okay," Terkel said, his voice distracted and tight.

"Terk?" Merk called from across the table. He got up and walked closer and sat across from Levi. "You don't sound too good, brother. What's up?"

"I'm fine," Terk said. "Or I will be. Right now, things are blown to shit."

"As in literally?" Merk asked.

"The entire group," Terk said, "they're all gone. I had a solid team of eight, and they're all gone."

"Dead?"

Several others stood to join them, gathered around Ice's phone. Levi stepped forward, his hand on Ice's shoulder. "Terk? Are they all dead?"

"No." Terk took a deep breath. "I'm not making sense. I'm sorry."

"Take it easy," Ice said, her voice calm and reassuring. "What do you mean, *they're all gone?*"

"All their abilities are gone," he said. "Something's happened to them. Somebody has deliberately removed whatever super senses they could utilize—or what we have been utilizing for the last ten years for the government." His tone was bitter. "When the US gov recently closed us down, they promised that our black ops department would never rise again, but I didn't expect them to attack us personally."

"What are you talking about?" Merk said in alarm, standing up now to stare at Ice's phone. "Are you in danger?"

"Maybe? I don't know," Terk said. "I need to find out exactly what the hell's going on."

"What can we do to help?" Ice asked.

Terk gave a broken laugh. "That's not why I'm calling. Well, it is, but it isn't."

Ice looked at Merk, who frowned, as he shook his head. Ice knew he and the others had heard Terk's stressed out tone and the completely confusing bits and pieces coming from his mouth. Ice said, "Terk, you're not making sense again. Take a breath and explain. Please. You're scaring me."

Terk took a long slow deep breath. "Tell Stone to open the gate," he said. "She's out there."

"Who's out there?" Levi asked, hopped up, looked outside, and shrugged.

"She's coming up the road now. You have to let her in."

"Who? Why?"

"*Because*," he said, "she's also harnessed with C-4."

"Jesus," Levi said, bolting to display the camera feeds to the big screen in the room. "Is it live?"

"It is, and she's been sent to you."

"Well, that's an interesting move," Ice said, her voice sharp, activating her comm to connect to Stone in the control room. "Who's after us?"

"I think it's rebels within the Iranian government. But it could be our own government. I don't know anymore," Terk snapped. "I also don't know how they got her so close to you. Or how they pinned your connection to me," he said. "I've been very careful."

"We can look after ourselves," Ice said immediately. "But who is this woman to you?"

"She's pregnant," he said, "so that adds to the intensity here."

"Understood. So who is the father? Is he connected somehow?"

There was silence on the other end.

Merk said, "Terk, talk to us."

"She's carrying my baby," Terk replied, his voice heavy.

Merk, his expression grim, looked at Ice, her face mirroring his shock. He asked, "How do you know her, Terk?"

"Brother, you don't understand," Terk said. "I've never met this woman before in my life." And, with that, the phone went dead.

Find Terkel's Team (Book #1) here!

To find out more visit Dale Mayer's website.

https://geni.us/DMTTDamonUniversal

Author's Note

Thank you for reading Flynn's Firecracker: Heroes for Hire, Book 5! If you enjoyed the book, please take a moment and leave a short review.

Dear reader,

I love to hear from readers, and you can contact me at my website: www.dalemayer.com or at my Facebook author page. To be informed of new releases and special offers, sign up for my newsletter or follow me on BookBub. And if you are interested in joining Dale Mayer's Reader Group, here is the Facebook sign up page.
http://geni.us/DaleMayerFBGroup

Cheers,
Dale Mayer

About the Author

Dale Mayer is a *USA Today* best-selling author, best known for her SEALs military romances, her Psychic Visions series, and her Lovely Lethal Garden cozy series. Her contemporary romances are raw and full of passion and emotion (Broken But ... Mending, Hathaway House series). Her thrillers will keep you guessing (Kate Morgan, By Death series), and her romantic comedies will keep you giggling (*It's a Dog's Life*, a stand-alone novella; and the Broken Protocols series, starring Charming Marvin, the cat).

Dale honors the stories that come to her—and some of them are crazy, break all the rules and cross multiple genres!

To go with her fiction, she also writes nonfiction in many different fields, with books available on résumé writing, companion gardening, and the US mortgage system. All her books are available in print and ebook format.

Connect with Dale Mayer Online

Dale's Website – www.dalemayer.com

Twitter – @DaleMayer

Facebook Page – geni.us/DaleMayerFBFanPage

Facebook Group – geni.us/DaleMayerFBGroup

BookBub – geni.us/DaleMayerBookbub

Instagram – geni.us/DaleMayerInstagram

Goodreads – geni.us/DaleMayerGoodreads

Newsletter – geni.us/DaleNews

Also by Dale Mayer

Published Adult Books:

Bullard's Battle

Ryland's Reach, Book 1

Cain's Cross, Book 2

Eton's Escape, Book 3

Garret's Gambit, Book 4

Kano's Keep, Book 5

Fallon's Flaw, Book 6

Quinn's Quest, Book 7

Bullard's Beauty, Book 8

Bullard's Best, Book 9

Terkel's Team

Damon's Deal, Book 1

Kate Morgan

Simon Says… Hide, Book 1

Hathaway House

Aaron, Book 1

Brock, Book 2

Cole, Book 3

Denton, Book 4

Elliot, Book 5

Finn, Book 6

Gregory, Book 7

Heath, Book 8

Iain, Book 9

Jaden, Book 10

Keith, Book 11

Lance, Book 12

Melissa, Book 13

Nash, Book 14

Owen, Book 15

Hathaway House, Books 1–3

Hathaway House, Books 4–6

Hathaway House, Books 7–9

The K9 Files

Ethan, Book 1

Pierce, Book 2

Zane, Book 3

Blaze, Book 4

Lucas, Book 5

Parker, Book 6

Carter, Book 7

Weston, Book 8

Greyson, Book 9

Rowan, Book 10

Caleb, Book 11

Kurt, Book 12

Tucker, Book 13

Harley, Book 14

The K9 Files, Books 1–2

The K9 Files, Books 3–4

The K9 Files, Books 5–6

The K9 Files, Books 7–8

The K9 Files, Books 9–10

The K9 Files, Books 11–12

Lovely Lethal Gardens

Arsenic in the Azaleas, Book 1

Bones in the Begonias, Book 2

Corpse in the Carnations, Book 3

Daggers in the Dahlias, Book 4

Evidence in the Echinacea, Book 5

Footprints in the Ferns, Book 6

Gun in the Gardenias, Book 7

Handcuffs in the Heather, Book 8

Ice Pick in the Ivy, Book 9

Jewels in the Juniper, Book 10

Killer in the Kiwis, Book 11

Lifeless in the Lilies, Book 12

Murder in the Marigolds, Book 13

Lovely Lethal Gardens, Books 1–2

Lovely Lethal Gardens, Books 3–4

Lovely Lethal Gardens, Books 5–6

Lovely Lethal Gardens, Books 7–8

Lovely Lethal Gardens, Books 9–10

Psychic Vision Series

Tuesday's Child

Hide 'n Go Seek

Maddy's Floor

Garden of Sorrow

Knock Knock...

Rare Find

Eyes to the Soul

Now You See Her

Shattered

Into the Abyss

Seeds of Malice

Eye of the Falcon

Itsy-Bitsy Spider

Unmasked

Deep Beneath

From the Ashes

Stroke of Death

Ice Maiden

Snap, Crackle...

Psychic Visions Books 1–3

Psychic Visions Books 4–6

Psychic Visions Books 7–9

By Death Series

Touched by Death

Haunted by Death

Chilled by Death

By Death Books 1–3

Broken Protocols – Romantic Comedy Series
Cat's Meow
Cat's Pajamas
Cat's Cradle
Cat's Claus
Broken Protocols 1-4

Broken and... Mending
Skin
Scars
Scales (of Justice)
Broken but... Mending 1-3

Glory
Genesis
Tori
Celeste
Glory Trilogy

Biker Blues
Morgan: Biker Blues, Volume 1
Cash: Biker Blues, Volume 2

SEALs of Honor
Mason: SEALs of Honor, Book 1
Hawk: SEALs of Honor, Book 2
Dane: SEALs of Honor, Book 3
Swede: SEALs of Honor, Book 4
Shadow: SEALs of Honor, Book 5
Cooper: SEALs of Honor, Book 6

Markus: SEALs of Honor, Book 7

Evan: SEALs of Honor, Book 8

Mason's Wish: SEALs of Honor, Book 9

Chase: SEALs of Honor, Book 10

Brett: SEALs of Honor, Book 11

Devlin: SEALs of Honor, Book 12

Easton: SEALs of Honor, Book 13

Ryder: SEALs of Honor, Book 14

Macklin: SEALs of Honor, Book 15

Corey: SEALs of Honor, Book 16

Warrick: SEALs of Honor, Book 17

Tanner: SEALs of Honor, Book 18

Jackson: SEALs of Honor, Book 19

Kanen: SEALs of Honor, Book 20

Nelson: SEALs of Honor, Book 21

Taylor: SEALs of Honor, Book 22

Colton: SEALs of Honor, Book 23

Troy: SEALs of Honor, Book 24

Axel: SEALs of Honor, Book 25

Baylor: SEALs of Honor, Book 26

Hudson: SEALs of Honor, Book 27

SEALs of Honor, Books 1–3

SEALs of Honor, Books 4–6

SEALs of Honor, Books 7–10

SEALs of Honor, Books 11–13

SEALs of Honor, Books 14–16

SEALs of Honor, Books 17–19

SEALs of Honor, Books 20–22

SEALs of Honor, Books 23–25

Heroes for Hire

Levi's Legend: Heroes for Hire, Book 1

Stone's Surrender: Heroes for Hire, Book 2

Merk's Mistake: Heroes for Hire, Book 3

Rhodes's Reward: Heroes for Hire, Book 4

Flynn's Firecracker: Heroes for Hire, Book 5

Logan's Light: Heroes for Hire, Book 6

Harrison's Heart: Heroes for Hire, Book 7

Saul's Sweetheart: Heroes for Hire, Book 8

Dakota's Delight: Heroes for Hire, Book 9

Michael's Mercy (Part of Sleeper SEAL Series)

Tyson's Treasure: Heroes for Hire, Book 10

Jace's Jewel: Heroes for Hire, Book 11

Rory's Rose: Heroes for Hire, Book 12

Brandon's Bliss: Heroes for Hire, Book 13

Liam's Lily: Heroes for Hire, Book 14

North's Nikki: Heroes for Hire, Book 15

Anders's Angel: Heroes for Hire, Book 16

Reyes's Raina: Heroes for Hire, Book 17

Dezi's Diamond: Heroes for Hire, Book 18

Vince's Vixen: Heroes for Hire, Book 19

Ice's Icing: Heroes for Hire, Book 20

Johan's Joy: Heroes for Hire, Book 21

Galen's Gemma: Heroes for Hire, Book 22

Zack's Zest: Heroes for Hire, Book 23

Bonaparte's Belle: Heroes for Hire, Book 24

Heroes for Hire, Books 1–3

Heroes for Hire, Books 4–6

Heroes for Hire, Books 7–9

Heroes for Hire, Books 10–12

Heroes for Hire, Books 13–15

SEALs of Steel

Badger: SEALs of Steel, Book 1

Erick: SEALs of Steel, Book 2

Cade: SEALs of Steel, Book 3

Talon: SEALs of Steel, Book 4

Laszlo: SEALs of Steel, Book 5

Geir: SEALs of Steel, Book 6

Jager: SEALs of Steel, Book 7

The Final Reveal: SEALs of Steel, Book 8

SEALs of Steel, Books 1–4

SEALs of Steel, Books 5–8

SEALs of Steel, Books 1–8

The Mavericks

Kerrick, Book 1

Griffin, Book 2

Jax, Book 3

Beau, Book 4

Asher, Book 5

Ryker, Book 6

Miles, Book 7

Nico, Book 8

Keane, Book 9

Lennox, Book 10

Gavin, Book 11

Shane, Book 12

Diesel, Book 13

Jerricho, Book 14

The Mavericks, Books 1–2

The Mavericks, Books 3–4

The Mavericks, Books 5–6

The Mavericks, Books 7–8

The Mavericks, Books 9–10

The Mavericks, Books 11–12

Collections

Dare to Be You...

Dare to Love...

Dare to be Strong...

RomanceX3

Standalone Novellas

It's a Dog's Life

Riana's Revenge

Second Chances

Published Young Adult Books:

Family Blood Ties Series

Vampire in Denial

Vampire in Distress

Vampire in Design

Vampire in Deceit

Vampire in Defiance

Vampire in Conflict

Vampire in Chaos

Vampire in Crisis

Vampire in Control

Vampire in Charge

Family Blood Ties Set 1–3

Family Blood Ties Set 1–5

Family Blood Ties Set 4–6

Family Blood Ties Set 7–9

Sian's Solution, A Family Blood Ties Series Prequel
Novelette

Design series

Dangerous Designs

Deadly Designs

Darkest Designs

Design Series Trilogy

Standalone

In Cassie's Corner

Gem Stone (a Gemma Stone Mystery)

Time Thieves

Published Non-Fiction Books:

Career Essentials

Career Essentials: The Résumé

Career Essentials: The Cover Letter

Career Essentials: The Interview

Career Essentials: 3 in 1

Printed in Great Britain
by Amazon

39536740R00136